HUNTRESS APPRENTICE

HUNTRESS APPRENTICE

HUNTRESS CLAN SAGA™ BOOK 2

JAMIE DAVIS

DISRUPTIVE IMAGINATION

Copyright © 2020 Jamie Davis
Cover Art by Jake @ J Caleb Design
http://jcalebdesign.com / jcalebdesign@gmail.com

LMBPN Publishing
PMB 196, 2540 South Maryland Pkwy
Las Vegas, NV 89109

First US Edition, January, 2020
eBook ISBN: 978-1-64202-693-1
Print ISBN: 978-1-64202-694-8

THE HUNTRESS APPRENTICE TEAM

Thanks to the Beta Readers
John Ashmore, Kelly O'Donnell, James Caplan, Larry
Omans, Rachel Beckford,

Thanks to the JIT Readers

Dave Hicks
Peter Manis
Diane L. Smith
Jeff Goode
Jeff Eaton
Dorothy Lloyd
Deb Mader

If I've missed anyone, please let me know!

Editor
The Skyhunter Editing Team

CHAPTER ONE

"Again."

Quinn groaned as she rose from the mat and squared herself to face Clark. The dark basement surrounded her in an oppressive silence. She heard nothing but her own breathing as she strained to draw in extra oxygen to try to recover some strength. She'd been down here for almost two hours sparring with Clark.

"I need a break," Quinn gasped.

"Again." Clark's voice carried the even, stern tone he'd used in every one of their training sessions.

No matter what Quinn did or said, he never seemed to lose his temper. It was one of the many things about her mentor that infuriated her. Nothing got under his skin.

Quinn lunged forward, then ducked to sweep Clark's legs out from under him while she tried to grab his shirt to pull him down to the mat beside her. The combination move was one he'd taught her earlier. She'd been struggling to get it right since.

He blocked her attempt to clutch him with a forward

thrust of his hands, separating her reaching arms before her hands could grab him.

In a desperate attempt to salvage something from the exchange, she continued her leg sweep. Maybe she could still topple him.

She should have known better.

Clark's hands drove forward in a continuation of the blocking maneuver, fingers together, so his hands formed dual spears that jabbed Quinn's chest. The blow knocked her off balance, and her leg sweep ended up propelling her around, her arms windmilling to recover before she landed on her back.

Quinn glared up at him.

The hunter stepped forward. The bare incandescent bulb in the rafters of the basement ceiling silhouetted him leaving his face in shadow. Quinn could see the barest hint of his headshake of disapproval.

"Dammit, Clark. How am I supposed to make this work when you're expecting me to try the exact move I'm using. It's the definition of futility."

Clark's answer carried a stern tone of admonishment. "You expect your opponents to just let you try out your moves on them without countering?"

"I did all right in my first fight with the demons." Quinn's anger rose to meet the hunter's disappointment.

"You were lucky. They'd been newly turned and possessed. They hadn't come into their full abilities in the new bodies yet."

Quinn shook her head. "I saved your butt, didn't I?"

He didn't take the bait. "Could you do it against a more prepared and skillful opponent?"

When Quinn didn't answer, Clark stepped back and gestured with one hand. "Get up. Again."

His dispassionate voice drove her anger to another level and sparked her to try something she hadn't used since the fight at the VirSync building almost a month before. When she concentrated on her strength and speed, a green bar appeared in her vision as she stared up at Clark. It was only at half-charge. Focusing her mind, she drew upon her stamina level to boost her abilities and climbed back to her feet.

Without waiting for Clark to gesture again, Quinn lunged forward, her enhanced speed and strength propelling her body at him. This time, when Clark's hands shot out to counter her attack, she moved so fast he was unable to bring his hands up before she'd breached his defenses.

For the first time, Quinn's fingers clutched the fabric of Clark's flannel shirt, her grasp tightening at the same instant her sweeping leg connected with his ankles.

To her delight, she glimpsed a hint of surprise in his eyes as she pulled him off-balance, causing him to topple to the floor beside her. She continued the move with a roll that should have ended with her atop him, pinning him to the mat.

Somehow, he got a knee raised in time to catch her in the chest as she descended on him. Before she could counter, Clark's leg straightened and propelled her over his head to land on the mat behind him.

Quinn's breath whooshed from her lungs, but she pushed through the pain and lack of air. Using her enhanced strength, she kicked her feet in the air and kipped back up to her feet again.

She spun around, hands at the ready to defend herself from any counterattack.

Clark had regained his feet as well and stood a few feet from her, crouched and ready. This time he nodded. "That was much better. You moved with a hunter's speed and agility that time."

"Yeah, but I can't do that all the time. I only have so much power to draw upon."

Clark's head cocked to one side. "What do you mean? You'll get tired like any person. Still, you'll be able to outlast most mundane opponents, and even most supernaturals if you're careful."

Quinn hadn't told anyone about her ability to use the VR skills she'd gained inside the VirSync training system in the real world. She'd tried to keep it a secret. This was the first time she'd used it in training with Clark.

"I have this thing I can sometimes do. It's sort of like a skill in a video game."

Clark stared at her and shook his head. He didn't understand what she'd said.

"When I first went into the VirSync system, I discovered I had certain abilities, the kind you'd gain in any sort of VR game setup. I could boost my strength to increase my speed and agility by drawing on my stamina stores."

"And you can do that here and now, outside their VR system?"

Quinn nodded.

"How long have you known you could do this?"

"Since the beginning. I used it in my fights in the

building when we were trying to escape. It's how I was able to match the demon-possessed strength of Cindy and the others."

"What else can you do besides this? Did you gain other skills?"

"I haven't tried them all, but I assume I can use the tracking ability and some of the other skills I had inside the training system."

"Why didn't you tell me about this sooner? This is important."

Quinn shrugged. "I didn't tell anyone because I was afraid it might mean I was still connected to their system somehow. I thought if I used it, they might be able to find out where we're hiding."

Clark shook his head. "Maybe that's true, but it could also explain why I can't get you to access your hunter attributes, despite all our training sessions."

"You helped me learn to use the magic in my amulet to hide in shadows. I wasn't inside the VR world then."

"Yes, but that was the power of the amulet. Those abilities are connected to it, at least initially, not to your hunter lineage. Somehow the magical interface of the amulet, coupled with the technology of the VR system, enabled you to access your hunter side inside the training scenarios and slayer hunts."

Clark reached out to the wooden post supporting the ceiling and tossed her a towel hanging from a hook there. "I need to talk to Miranda about this. Maybe we've been going about your training all wrong. Come on upstairs."

Quinn caught the towel as Clark turned toward the steps leading to the main floor of the farmhouse. She pressed the soft terrycloth against her face, wiping her sweat-soaked skin. Her dark hair, damp with sweat, hung about her face, clinging to her cheeks and forehead. The dark locks had started out pulled back into a ponytail, but all the training of the last two hours had shaken most of it loose. She'd given up trying to keep it in place between bouts.

The training here day in and day out would have worn her down, but Quinn kept her focus on her ultimate goal, inspired by that mysterious voice she had first heard barely a month before.

"Welcome, and well done, my daughter, my Quinn, my new huntress," the woman's voice had said in her mind.

To Quinn, it hinted at something she'd long dreamed of —a family. Now she saw their small group, the four of them, as the beginning of a new family, one she could build to become whatever she wanted it to be. But it all hinged on her learning the hunter skills from Clark and matching them until she became a true huntress, one with a full clan behind her and not just an Initiate.

She headed for the open wooden steps leading up to the farmhouse's kitchen. Clark had brought her and Taylor here, along with the witch, Miranda. He chose this secluded location as a hideout after their escape from the VirSync building.

The property was located about twenty minutes north of Baltimore, where a few patches of farmland still remained amidst the sprawl of housing developments and businesses. This particular farm was vacant, and according to the sign at the end of the long lane leading out to the main road, up for auction in a few more weeks. When that happened, they'd have to relocate.

Clark's animated voice met her as Quinn reached the kitchen. It differed from the passionless monotone he used most of the time. "I think we had a breakthrough just now. Quinn did something I haven't seen her do before."

Miranda smiled at Quinn as she entered the room and turned back to Clark. "What kind of something?"

"She finally displayed some of the hunter strength and speed I've been trying to unlock in her. Usually, we begin training young initiates at the age of ten. That way, when they hit puberty and their abilities manifest, they're prepared to access them through the hours of meditation and training we've given them. With Quinn, I had to try something different."

Quinn stared at Clark and said, "That was why you kept me down there for hours every day? To force me to release some sort of hidden abilities?"

Clark nodded. "I didn't know any other way. If you remember, I tried to get you to meditate. You laughed it off and wouldn't give it a serious try. Given your prior martial arts training, I figured I could use a different sort of focused attention to spark you to release your skills."

Quinn began to snap out an angry reply, but Miranda cut her off. "So, then, I guess your plan worked?"

"Yes and no," Clark said. "At least, not the way I expected it to. I think I understand now why I couldn't unlock her abilities myself. It had already happened inside the VirSync VR system. The combination of technology and magic in their VR rig had already done it."

Quinn huffed and said, "It could've saved us both a lot of time and pain if you'd only told me what you were trying to do. You know, you're really failing at the mentoring gig. It's like you've never done anything like this before."

"I haven't."

"What?" Quinn and Miranda replied in unison.

"I was barely an apprentice hunter when the purges began twenty years ago. I only escaped being discovered and killed through blind luck."

"But I thought..." Quinn began.

Clark shook his head. "I'd been through most of the training, but I hadn't reached the level of Master Hunter, where I'd have my own initiates to train. The rest of the clan members were killed before then."

Quinn's anger bubbled up. "You lied to me, Clark. You told me you could train me to become the huntress I was destined to be."

"And I have. It just took us longer to get there, partly because you didn't tell me everything you could already do."

"I was afraid to," Quinn said. "I told you, I was afraid they could track me if I used the skill outside their building or VR setup."

Clark shook his head. "If that was the case, why'd you use it today?"

"Because I got so pissed off, I didn't care anymore. You stood there with that smug look on your face while you countered everything I could throw at you. I had to take you down just once."

Miranda laughed. "You two need to come up with a better way to communicate with each other. All you do is fight and argue. It sounds like this could have been solved with a little one-on-one communication."

Taylor, Quinn's best friend, walked into the kitchen with an empty red plastic cup in her hand. Her wireless headphones hung around her neck. "Don't stop fighting on my account. I'm just here to get some water. I've been listening from the dining room, and the whole thing is super entertaining. Your daily training arguments almost make it bearable to be stuck here in the middle of nowhere."

The mousy blonde got a pitcher of filtered water from the fridge and filled her cup, then took a sip. "What's the issue today? Is our trainee huntress still not progressing to your man-standards?"

Clark ignored Taylor's dig and turned to Quinn. "Go get a shower and cool down. We can talk more about this when you're finished. This is a breakthrough. I wish it happened sooner, but at least it happened."

Quinn started to say something but decided Clark's attempt at defusing the situation was probably for the best. Besides, she just felt grimy. Flipping the towel up over her shoulder, Quinn nodded and headed to the hallway by the front door and the stairs to the second floor. A shower would feel good after two grueling hours of hard work.

CHAPTER TWO

Clark waited for Quinn to leave and start up the stairs before he spoke, his voice lowered so it didn't carry beyond the kitchen. "I think this will change everything. She has no idea how close I was to giving up on getting her training to work. Even if she was the daughter of a hunter clan member, I don't know of any precedent for beginning training of someone her age."

Taylor shook her head. "I'm missing something, what happened today that's different?"

"I couldn't unlock her hunter abilities because she'd already done it, we just didn't know it."

Taylor laughed. "I told you last week you were approaching this all wrong. Quinn is special. I've always known it, as long as we've been best friends. She always does things her own way, and they have a habit of working out. How did you find out she'd already broken through your little hunter wall?"

Clark ignored her attempted dig. "It came up downstairs just now. I'm not entirely sure where we go from here, but I think I'll need your help to figure it out."

"Mine? Why me?" Taylor asked.

"Because her breakthrough happened when she was at VirSync inside the VR training system."

Taylor seemed confused. Clark continued, "I'm guessing it's something to do with her wearing the amulet coupled with the magic and technology interface they used to send you, Quinn, and the other candidates out as slayers. I was hoping you and Miranda would be able to explain it to me. She's our resident witch, and you're—well, I guess you're our tech witch."

A broad grin crossed Taylor's face. "'Tech witch.' I like that. It's a whole lot better than 'garden-variety hacker.'"

Clark chuckled. Taylor's inclusion in their little band had been the one part he'd initially resisted. He didn't see how she was going to contribute until Quinn got her hooked up on a used laptop he had bought from a pawn shop on one of his regular runs into the city for supplies. Since none of them could go home to get their things, it was the best he could do, and she said she needed it to get them all some semblance of civilization in their new home.

She'd managed to fire it up, get them free internet from the cable box at the end of the lane, and even managed to hack into the power grid and get the power turned back on.

The real bonus was how she diffused tense situations with her quirky humor and ever-present positive attitude. Perpetually perky people like Taylor bugged him, but as soon as he saw the effect she had on Quinn, Miranda, and even him, he realized she was an asset to the team.

"Hopefully, you'll live up to the moniker, kid. Now that I've figured out how to break through to Quinn's inherent abilities, I need you and Miranda to come through in a big way."

Miranda stood, pouring a fresh cup of coffee from the old drip coffee maker left on the counter when the previous residents moved out. "I don't know what you want me to do. I don't know anything about training a new hunter. You're the expert there."

"I can handle the training end, but I need you to come up with a way to duplicate the VR gear VirSync used to create their system. It had both tech and magical components. I think you two are going to have to work together to get it done."

Taylor shook her head. "I'm not usually the one to crap on anyone's ideas, but what you're asking is nearly impossible. I saw their system and understood what they were doing. At least I thought I did before I discovered they were using magic against us, too. They had top-level equipment and customized gear much better than anything you could find in a random pawn shop in the city."

"She's right, Clark," Miranda said. "Not to mention the issues we'd have duplicating the magic spells they used to get their system to even work. I wouldn't know where to start conjuring something like that."

"Oh, I can help with that," Taylor said.

Both Clark and Miranda turned to stare at her. Clark said. "You just got done saying you couldn't do anything to help."

"I didn't say that. I said I didn't have the gear to do it

and didn't think it would be easy to find. The how of doing it is different. I got a pretty good look at the code they were using once when they left me alone in the control room for my VR suite. I couldn't resist scrolling down to see how their system was coded. I never forget anything I read. Most of it is right up here." Taylor tapped her head with one finger.

Miranda shook her head. "But that's the code, the computer stuff. How does that help me come up with a spell?"

"Easy. There were things in the lines of code that didn't make any sense to me at the time. Now that I've had some time to think about it, especially after talking with you about the nature of magic, I think I know what those extra nonsense lines of code meant."

"You think they were some sort of spell written into the software?" Clark asked.

Taylor nodded and gestured to Miranda. "You told me last week that magical energy harnessed something somehow related to the magnetic field of the earth running along hidden lines in the earth around us."

Miranda nodded. "Yes, ley lines."

"I did some research because I didn't understand how these hidden energy lines worked. I figured out they're kind of like Longitude and Latitude lines, just more chaotic. As soon as I figured that out, the lines of code in my head kind of figured themselves out."

Miranda smiled. "I think I see where you're going. I couldn't figure out how VirSync was teleporting the slayers physically out into the real world while still tapping into their VR world skills. If the code referred to ley line coordinates, they could be used to target a specific location on the map. That would enable the spell caster to send the slayers to that location while inside the training system."

"Exactly," Taylor said, a beaming smile spread across her face.

Clark looked from one woman to the other and back again. "I don't understand. So can you recreate the VR system they used on you all to create the slayer assassins or not?"

Taylor and Miranda both nodded.

Miranda said, "If what Taylor says is true, then it's possible we could pool our efforts together to create a similar effect, at least magically."

Taylor's smile turned into a frown. "The magic is the easy part. We still don't have the right equipment to do what we need to do. It'll take way more than just a two-year-old laptop to do what we need them to do. I can't modify that hunk of junk to do anything approaching the computing power we'd need. I might be able to modify my old system at home if you'd let me go home and get it."

Clark jumped in. "No. No going back to our homes, for any of us. It would be too risky, even for me, and I don't think they have any tracking info on me. It's definitely out of the question for you and Quinn. There has to be a way we can get the gear you need to do what is necessary."

"Sure, if you have fifty thousand dollars and a dedicated team of assembly techs," Taylor quipped. "What we need is gear from VirSync itself."

"How are we supposed to do that?" Miranda asked. "We barely made it out the last time we were there."

"I know," Taylor said. "It's impossible to do. I was just

trying to explain how specialized their gear is. Too bad we can't get back in there for a few minutes. That's all I'd need inside one of the store-rooms in the VR training wing. I saw one of them while I was there. There were several older versions of the VR rig in it. I'm sure we could get everything we need there and no one would even miss it. It's outdated technology from their standpoint."

Clark started to say "no" to the idea, but he thought about how hard it had been to train Quinn so far. It had taken a month to have the single breakthrough she'd had. There was something extraordinary about her. He could feel it deep inside. He also could feel that her abilities would only come to fruition if he could get her trained in time to make it count.

"We might not have a choice," Clark said to himself in a low voice.

"What was that?" Miranda asked. "You're not actually considering going back in there to try some sort of heist, are you?

Clark shrugged. "It's worth thinking about. Quinn needs this gear to train. I don't know why or how, but she does." He glanced at Taylor. "How much gear are we talking about here? Are we going to need a big truck, or is it something one or two of us could carry out by hand?"

Taylor considered his question for a few seconds before answering. "I guess we could carry what I'd need with two people. It would be heavy, but I think we could handle it. It would be easier if we had a cart or something like that."

"Okay, so if we can get in there, is there a way for you to watch as we go in and tell us what you need us to grab?"

Taylor crossed her arms. "I suppose that means you're not taking me along?"

"It's possible for Quinn and me to slip inside without being seen. I have no way to hide you."

Taylor hmphed. "Fine. I suppose I could come up with a remote wireless camera system you could wear. Then I could help you pick out what I needed from the pile. I'd have to be pretty close by, though, because we can't use a long-distance connection over the web. They'd surely detect that. A locally generated signal might be able to slip past their systems since it wouldn't be on a standard Wi-Fi or cellular signal carrier."

"I have no idea what you just said," Clark replied.

"Of course not. That's because I'm the tech witch, and you're not." Taylor laughed. "Yes, I can rig up a system to communicate with you so you can get the things I need. I'll need a few more things from that pawn shop of yours and maybe a run to the mega-mart to get a few final items."

Clark smiled. "Good. Make your list. I'll make a run out to shop. You start putting the camera rig together. Once we have that working, we can figure out a way to get back inside the VirSync grounds."

Miranda shook her head. "You know they'll have plugged any of the gaps they had in their perimeter wards."

"I'm counting on it," Clark replied. "I want them to think they've got nothing to worry about. Then, when you and our little tech witch here hacks the magical and technological security systems, they won't know what hit them. Put your heads together and come up with a game plan. I'll go out and get the shopping done as soon as Taylor makes her list."

Taylor already had her phone out and was tapping away with her thumbs. It was one of the burner phones she'd hacked to work together in a local network with the ones the others carried.

A few seconds later, a buzz in Clark's pocket told him he had a text. He pulled out the phone and tapped the message to open it. His eyebrows shot up. "This is everything? You're sure you can make what you need from this?"

"Yep," Taylor said. "I've got this. Don't worry. You've got Taylor, the teenaged tech witch, on your side."

Clark resisted a groan, grabbing his car keys and wondering if he'd somehow created a monster with his label for the girl. Too late now, though. He hoped she lived up to the name once he'd filled her strange shopping list.

CHAPTER THREE

Quinn rubbed the towel into her long dark hair, trying to wring the remaining water from it as she stood in front of the scratched and stained bathroom mirror. She couldn't help but notice the dark circles under her eyes. Clark's daily training bouts had taken a toll on her. Even with her ability to heal faster than most people, each night, her body felt like she'd been run over by a city bus until she got a good night's sleep.

She knew she should be happier with her accomplishment. This was the first time she'd had any success during training bouts against her teacher. His infuriating passionless glare irked her. He drove her to press so hard to succeed that she dug into reserves in her unenhanced human stamina she hadn't known she'd had before.

Quinn sighed.

Perhaps that had been the point. Her lacrosse coach in high school had driven her harder than she thought she could take on more than one occasion. It usually led her to a standout play and team victory. She didn't want to admit Clark's training regimen might actually have some merit.

She heard his old sedan's engine fire up outside, and she walked to the window. Clark drove down the tree-lined lane to the main road a quarter-mile away. Where was he going?

Quinn hung the towel on the rod by the shower to dry and got dressed. She pulled her hair up into a high ponytail to keep it up off her neck and headed downstairs. Miranda and Taylor sat at the dining room table, huddled over the laptop, chatting about something.

"Hey, where did Clark head off to? He just went grocery shopping yesterday. Did he forget something?"

Taylor looked up from the screen and smiled. "No, he's doing some shopping for me. We're all going on a mission to break into the VirSync building again."

"Why in hell would we want to do that?" Quinn asked.

"Because," Taylor replied, "there's stuff we need there to recreate the VR system. Clark thinks we need it so you can continue your training the right way."

Quinn raised up her hand to stop her friend before she said anything else. "What kind of crazy idea did you all hatch while I was upstairs in the shower? I think I should have been consulted about anything like sending me back into that damned VR system."

Miranda smiled and said, "It's fine, Quinn. Clark's idea makes sense. You'll progress in your training faster using a VR system. This time it'll be different. He asked Taylor and me to try to recreate something like it here. You won't be in their system, you'll be in ours. I promise you'll be safe."

Taylor nodded. "Miranda and I were just going through

some lines of the VirSync code I memorized. I'm showing her the references to specific spell magic interspersed throughout the programming. With that, I'm sure we can make it work."

"Taylor's right, Quinn," Miranda said. "I think I can extrapolate the spells they used to send people into their training system. If it works, we could create training scenarios with Clark that should allow you to unlock more skills to add to your huntress arsenal."

Quinn smiled at that last bit. Miranda understood about Quinn's insistence on using the feminine form of hunter when referring to herself. Clark resisted, of course, but he was just a pig-headed man. He'd get over it, especially if the rest of them used the correct terminology when referring to Quinn. He kept insisting that "back in the day," the hunters who were women never referred to themselves that way. Her answer every time he mentioned it was to tell him it was a different world than it was eighteen years ago.

"It would be nice to have an easier time accomplishing things during the training sessions. He puts me through hell when I don't succeed."

Taylor laughed. "I wouldn't count on that. I think he lives for new ways to come up with training that hurts."

Taylor had been doing some self-defense training with Clark when he was finished with Quinn every day. She'd seen her friend limping around in the evenings enough to know he was as hard on Taylor as he was on his huntress pupil. It was like he only had one setting, and that was at maximum—hardcore difficulty level for anything he did.

Quinn returned her friend's chuckle, "I can hear him

saying, 'Train hard to win hard' or something like that. Seriously, he needs to take a break. I never see him take any downtime."

Miranda shook her head. "He can't afford to. He's the last of his kind, or one of the last. If he doesn't take every opportunity when it comes, he's setting himself up to lose. For him, losing means death. I get the feeling he's got something he has to do or make up for, like survivor's guilt or something. He has that sort of drive in his eyes. I've seen it in a few mages I've known over the years."

Quinn glanced at Miranda and tried to assess her age. The woman looked to be in her mid-twenties, but when she said things like that, it made Quinn wonder if she was older than she appeared. On more than one occasion, she'd considered asking outright but had changed her mind before she did. Miranda still had an air of sadness and loss around her. Ever since the deaths of her coven at the hands of the VirSync slayers, it seemed like she expected to die, too.

"How long is Clark supposed to be?" Quinn asked.

Taylor said, "I gave him a list, but he should be able to find most of what I need in the bigger stores around this area. I don't think he has to go into the city, or at least not all the way downtown. He can get the things on the list around here. That'll give Miranda and me time to nail down some of the code gaps I have in what I saw while I was a candidate at the company. That way, I'll have a better idea of what I need him to collect for us once he gets inside the company grounds."

"I still can't believe he wants to go back in there. He spent the last month trying to keep me away, despite my desire to go and try to save some of the other candidates. Now that I'm over it, he seems to have finally given in. It's a little frustrating."

"In all fairness, honey," Taylor said. "I've always been better at convincing people to do what I wanted than you. Miranda helped convince him, too."

"Hey, don't drag me in on this. It's all on you."

Taylor laughed. "Fine. I'm a big girl. I can handle the responsibility. Now, let's get back to work on this. I want to have a wish list of what we need based on what you and I find in the code before Clark gets back."

Quinn left the two of them alone in the dining room and headed into the kitchen to make herself a sandwich. Training always left her starving until she recharged with some food.

She sat down with her plate at the small round kitchen table and flipped through her phone's news feed while she ate.

Quinn was still sitting there when Clark came through the back door with a brown cardboard box held in front of him.

He jerked his head back toward the door. "Hey, Quinn. There are a few more bags from the mega-mart in the back seat. Can you go get them?"

"Sure." Quinn got up and went outside to Clark's car. She retrieved the two large plastic bags from the back seat. When she returned inside, she heard the others in the dining room and carried the bags in there.

"Put them on the table, Quinn," Taylor said. "Clark said he got everything on my list, but I want to go through the stuff myself to be sure."

Quinn set the two bags on the table beside the big open box. It looked like it was filled with a strange assortment of odds and ends. She'd seen a soldering iron in one of the bags she'd carried in.

Clark reached into the box and pulled out two white boxes with cords wrapped around them. "Are we really going to need these? The guy at the pawnshop tried to congratulate me on the new baby until I told him he was way off the mark."

Taylor smiled. "Oh, the video baby monitors? Yeah, they're super important. They're the linchpin of the whole set up. I'm going to use them to create a two-way video communication system so you can show me everything you see while I'm outside the complex."

Clark shook his head. "I didn't know they'd reach that far."

"They reach farther than you'd think, but you're right. I need to modify them, which is why I had the other stuff on the list. We should be able to increase the range significantly, at least for short-term transmission. I have some ideas about how we could use them with the VR system, too."

Miranda's eyebrows shot up. "You think we can use them to see what's going on inside the VR world?"

"I don't see why not. If we can transport a person in there and have them physically show up in this world, I don't see why we can't send something tangible with them and have a signal come back to use. I'll have to tweak it a little, I'm sure, but it should work, in theory. I'm surprised the VirSync folks didn't think it up, too. That would have

24

really jacked up your ability to evade them, though, so I'm glad they didn't."

Quinn said, "Philip and Velma were always talking about planned upgrades. It could have been something on their list for all we know."

"True," Taylor said. "I guess if we ever run into any of them again and they're wearing body cams, we'll know."

Clark put the two baby monitors back in the box. "How long will it take you to do what you need to do?"

Taylor looked over the assembled gear and looked up at the ceiling for a few seconds. "I think I can have it done by tomorrow if everything works the way I think it will."

Clark nodded. "Good, get on it. I want to continue Quinn's training using the VR gear as soon as possible."

"You know, once we get the stuff from VirSync, I'll need several days or even weeks to put together a usable system."

Miranda nodded to agree with Taylor. "Plus, we don't know how long it will take us to get the spells exactly right to meld with the technology. We can't rush this, Clark."

He pressed his lips together in a grim line. "I don't think we'll have a choice. Once we break back into their perimeter, they'll know we're still out here gunning for them. I'm sure they'll redouble their efforts to track us down. We'll need to be ready to fight fire with fire of our own. That means we need a way to get Quinn and maybe even me into the VR system as soon as possible."

Taylor nodded. "I'll do the best I can. Beyond that, it'll take more than a little luck."

"Understood," Clark said. "First things first. Get the video transmission gear together so we can get what you need from inside. Quinn and I will put our heads together based on what we know about the facility and try to come up with a plan to break in without getting caught. It's time to see if our young huntress is up to facing down some of her demons again."

"Don't worry about me, Clark. I'll be ready." Quinn met his gaze, keeping her eyes steady to show her resolve.

Clark smiled and shook his head. "You're assuming they won't have beefed things up to make it harder for us. They've met us once. They won't take us for granted again. Now that they know there are real hunters out there looking for them, they can't afford to let their guard down. They'll be ready for us, and that means we have to be ready for anything they can throw at us. Come on, let's get some more reps in tonight before dinner."

Quinn stifled a groan. She'd just showered.

Clark stared at her from the top of the basement steps until she started to his way. As soon as she did, he started back down to the training area in the basement. There was no break for her while the others tried to assemble the gear. He was going to run her through her paces again and again until she dropped or got it right.

CHAPTER FOUR

The following night, after another full day in the basement, training, Quinn stood in the kitchen while Taylor rigged the power cable to the battery in the fanny pack at her waist. She taped it around her arm so the cord remained in place when she moved. It ran up over her shoulder and down her back to the black nylon pack. It held the batteries and electronic guts for the live video rig the tech witch devised over the last day and a half.

"Shrug your shoulders up and down a few times so I can see if it stays in place. I don't want it coming loose if you get in a fight." Taylor took a step back to watch as Quinn did as she was told.

After a few training moves with her arms and legs, Quinn stopped and said, "It seems like everything is staying put."

"Good, I think that's got it, then. How's the set up on Clark looking, Miranda?"

Over in the opposite side of the kitchen, Miranda

crouched behind the hunter, settling the fanny pack in place after attaching the cable harness that ran to the camera mounted on Clark's chest. "I think I've almost got it worked out..."

The witch stood and looked over the collection of wires and nylon straps that made up the camera rig and harness. "I think we're good here, Taylor. Not too bad if I say so myself."

"I'll echo that," Quinn said. She twisted at the waist to test the harness holding the camera and cables settled on her shoulders and around her chest. "It was a great idea to use the nylon tow straps you found in the barn to create the harness."

"That was all Miranda," Taylor said. "She cut and stitched them together, so they fit both of you just right."

"You could've done it, too," Miranda said.

Taylor laughed. "Yeah, but I would've totally used duct tape instead of taking the time to stitch it with upholstery thread to make sure it stayed in place."

Clark growled low in his throat. "Enough self-congratulations. We've got a lot to do tonight, and it's going to be dangerous enough without you all giggling about it all night."

"We're not giggling, Clark," Quinn corrected him. "Besides, we're ready to go when you are."

"Then let's load up. It's late enough that no one should be still around from the normal day shift workers. That should leave just the night guards and janitors for us to avoid."

"As long as there aren't any demon-possessed people

wandering around," Taylor cautioned. She looked at Clark. "You did say they no longer slept like normal people once they took over a body."

"They don't," Clark said. "The demons only see them as vessels to be used up. They'll run their human bodies into the ground if it suits them. Also, they don't suffer from the same physical and psychological issues as humans who undergo sleep deprivation." He turned and pushed open the farmhouse's back door and walked out onto the porch with the others following right behind him.

Quinn glanced up at the bright moon lighting up the night sky above them. It was somewhere around three-quarters full. Only a few dark clouds floated around it. She climbed into the back seat of Clark's old sedan with Taylor. Clark and Miranda sat in the front. Clark drove.

"You all set?" Quinn asked Taylor.

The hacker smiled and patted the large duffel bag on the seat next to her. "The wireless monitors from the baby cameras are in here so we can watch each of you on your own separate camera feeds. I'll see what you see. Miranda and I tested them all the way out to the end of the lane, and the feed was crystal clear. That's almost a quarter-mile. I figure we should be fine if we're able to park just outside the perimeter wall near the VirSync compound."

"Good. Hopefully, we can get that close." Quinn said. She held up crossed fingers and Taylor smiled, matching the gesture.

Clark drove down the lane and headed for the inter-state, taking them back to the city.

Everyone fell silent as they continued to drive toward

the company compound, each of them lost in their own private thoughts about their chances of success.

Excitement gripped Quinn. She wasn't apprehensive at all. This was her first opportunity to get out of the farmhouse and do something constructive in over a month. They'd all been virtual prisoners since their escape. Part of her wanted a chance to face off against demon-possessed Cindy or even Myles Hickman again. She needed to get back at them for all the lives they'd affected with their evil plan. Besides the people they'd had their slayers kill while inside the VR system, who knew how many of the remaining candidates had been brought down to that cavern for demonic conversion?

She looked out the window, surprised to see they were already on the road that ran past the VirSync headquarters. It hadn't taken them long to get to where they were going. She had no idea where the farmhouse was, but apparently, it wasn't that far from their enemies.

There was little to no traffic this time of night, and they made good time. They approached the VirSync compound as the only car on the darkened road.

"Something's wrong," Miranda said when they were nearing the last intersection before the company's walled enclosure started.

"What is it?" Clark asked.

"The magic emanating from the area ahead of us feels weaker, not stronger. That makes no sense."

Clark nodded as he remained stopped at the intersection. He leaned forward, peering over the steering wheel at the darkness ahead of them. "Are you sure?"

"As sure as I can be. Unless they've come up with a way to mask things better than anything I've seen, there would be a much stronger presence from the wards than I'm feeling."

"Everyone, keep your eyes open," Clark said. "I don't know what this means, but if you see anything unusual, call out. I'll start down past the main entrance. We can just drive by and see what's up without stopping. Once we get a look past the gate, we can turn around and come back so we can find the best place to try to breach the wall."

Quinn turned to look out her window as Clark drove them down the road to her former employer's company headquarters. The tall concrete and wrought iron wall surrounding the compound began on their left as soon as Clark passed through the intersection.

Miranda spoke in a quiet, steady voice as they drove along. "The wards are definitely weaker than they were. In some places, they've faded completely. These things need to be reinforced periodically in order for them to be effective. Left alone, the magic quickly dissipates."

Quinn nodded as they got closer because the witch was correct. Something was different. Quinn used to come here at night to work with the other candidates. What she saw now wasn't right. It took her a few seconds to figure out what it was.

Taylor beat her to it. "The lights are out. It should be brighter."

Quinn nodded. "Yeah, she's right. The parking lot for employees is behind this part of the wall. The lot's street-lamps in that part of the facility should be lit up this time of night. They're not. We'd see the glow over the wall if they were."

"We're almost to the entrance," Clark said. "Try to catch a look past the gate with a camera and see if you can spot the main building from the road."

Taylor slid over to see past Quinn out her window as the two of them watched from the seat behind Clark.

This time Quinn spotted the changes first. "There's no guard, and the shack by the gate is empty. And look! The gate is open."

Clark kept driving by as they all tried to see what was up with the company compound. Quinn couldn't see much past the entrance even with the gate open. The main building sat back away from the road far enough that she could only see the upper floors. The windows there were dark, but that was to be expected this time of night.

After they passed by, Clark looked at Miranda. "Anything?"

The witch shook her head. "It's the same as I said before. The wards have faded. I can't sense any increased magical presence at all. It's like it's deserted."

"That can't be the case. Why would they do something like that?" Clark asked. "They ran us off and still had every advantage over us."

A thought occurred to Quinn. "Yeah, but do they know that? We managed to escape and defeated or even killed several of them on the way out. They thought all the hunters were dead until we showed up. Maybe that spooked them to the point that they shut down operations completely."

"Unlikely," Clark replied. "Still, you might be partly right. My guess is they just moved to a new location."

"Turn around and go back to the main entrance," Quinn said. "If they're gone, we'll be able to enter and drive all the way out to the main building without anyone stopping us."

"That's pretty bold, Quinn," Clark said, then without warning, turned the wheel, executing a U-turn that took them back the way they came. "But, as they say, fortune favors the bold."

Soon they were back at the main gate. "Here goes," Clark said as he goosed the accelerator and pulled the beat-up sedan up the sloped driveway past the main entrance and into the VirSync compound.

As they drove up to the front of the darkened structure of the main office building, Quinn shook her head. "They're completely gone. There's no one here at all."

"Don't assume that," Clark warned. "It could be a trap."

"A trap they left like this every night for a month in hopes we'd come back?" Quinn replied. "That doesn't make sense. It looks like they've pulled out and left this place vacant."

Clark looked at Miranda.

She nodded. "I don't sense anything. When we were here last, there was a strong presence of magic. It's just not here anymore. There's barely a trickle of magic around anymore."

Quinn pointed to the circle driveway that pulled up to the main entrance doors. "Pull up there. I'll get out and try the doors."

Clark shrugged and drove up to the doors. Quinn and

Taylor both hopped out and walked to the building's entrance. Quinn checked the doors as she peered past the glass door into the darkened entryway. If the building was occupied, there should be a security guard seated at the desk midway across the broad open lobby. The tall desk sat empty. Quinn pulled the door handles with both hands.

"They're locked, but the building looks deserted."

Behind her, the car's engine stopped. As she continued to peer into the dark, deserted lobby, Clark and Miranda came over and joined the two teens by the entrance.

"You're right. It looks like they bugged out," Clark said. "That doesn't mean there isn't still some danger here. This was a place of evil power, and there could be residual magic or even physical traps around. Everyone should stay on their toes."

Quinn and Taylor nodded. Clark looked at the door and waved a hand past the locks at the top and bottom of the doors, his fingers forming a sort of symbol. An audible click sounded each time.

"How'd you do that?" Quinn asked.

"You should be able to learn to do it. Maybe you will if I can figure out a way to train you. That's why we're here, remember?"

Taylor leaned against the glass, staring in at the darkened lobby. "Do you think they left anything behind for us to grab?"

Clark shrugged. "No way to know until we get in there and look around. I'll go first, then Miranda. You two come behind us. The two of us will try to detect any trouble before we stumble upon anything. You two keep your eyes open anyway. Say something if you see anything that doesn't look right."

Quinn and Taylor nodded and came forward to follow the other two inside as Clark pulled open the door and stepped into the building. The two girls walked in behind the others, letting the heavy glass door shut behind them.

CHAPTER FIVE

The farther Quinn and the others went into the facility, the surer they were the company headquarters had been vacated in a hurry.

"Look," Taylor said as they passed the hallway with the VR training rooms. "Most of the computer equipment was left behind in the outer control rooms. They cleaned out the VR gear and specialized electronics, but they left the basic computers. It makes sense. They can buy those anywhere."

Clark nodded. "That means they moved the operation to send out the slayers. They only took the stuff they needed to set up again in a new location. Is there anything here you can use?"

Taylor shrugged, "This is good stuff, but nothing here is unique. If we have time, I could grab a few monitors, but that's it."

"Okay," Clark said. "We'll keep looking. Where were those storerooms you mentioned?"

Taylor pointed down the hall.

Quinn nodded. She knew the ones Taylor meant from the description she gave. "They're down there past the locker rooms. I can show you. Taylor, grab what you need here with Miranda while Clark and I go and get the storerooms unlocked. We'll wait for you there."

Taylor nodded, and Miranda held back to remain with Taylor.

Quinn followed Clark down the hall as he led the way. "It's not far. Just before the end of the hall."

"Stay behind me, just in case they left some sort of magical trap behind," Clark cautioned.

"I'm fine. I've got my amulet."

"Don't count on that too much, Quinn. It's a crutch. Your brain is your best defense. It's better to use the amulet like an emergency backup parachute. You don't want to use it because it means things are super messed up and out of your control at that point."

Quinn nodded, but her hand drifted up to brush the amulet hanging around her neck. It had protected her and warned her ever since she could remember. She didn't like to think she relied on it too much. It had been such a constant in her life. She followed Clark's instructions to stay behind him, though.

There were no traps, and the two of them reached the storeroom without incident. Clark unlocked it using his spell or ability to do so. She was unsure which it was.

Quinn pulled the door open and saw a ten-foot square room full of random electronics and gear. The stuff was stacked on shelves and filled most of the floor, too.

"Do you know what Taylor needs?" Clark asked.

"No, she's the techie. She should be here soon."

"I'm here, I'm here," Taylor said.

Taylor and Miranda pushed a small wheeled cart down the hall. A pair of computer monitors and a tower computer system sat on the lower of the cart's two shelves.

"Did you get enough?" Quinn asked with a grin. This must be like Christmas in July for her friend.

"When Miranda found the cart and knowing we have the car pulled right up out front, I figured there wasn't any reason not to grab anything that might be helpful to us."

Clark pointed to the dark storage room. "What about in here? Is this the stuff you needed?"

Taylor walked up and pulled out a flashlight. She aimed it at the jumble of equipment stashed in the closet and smiled. "This is perfect. Miranda, pull the cart over by the entrance. I should be able to get everything I want to grab to fit onto the cart."

Five minutes later, they rolled the overloaded cart back through the lobby to the entrance. As they did, Quinn looked back over her shoulder at the double doors. They led to the long hallway she'd taken to get to the basement level and the caverns below when rescuing Taylor a month ago. Her thoughts went back to everything that happened that night.

While Quinn was lost in thought, Clark, Taylor, and Miranda unloaded the cart, stashing everything in the sedan's trunk.

Clark nodded and shut the trunk lid. "Let's get going before someone shows up to check on the place."

"We can't leave yet," Quinn said.

"Why not?" Clark asked.

"The Ruby Heart was down there the last time we were

here. There's a chance it might still be down there now, hidden where I left it. If they didn't find it, that thing's a powerful artifact, and we might be able to use it to help us in our search for VirSync and their new operation."

Miranda shook her head. "It's an object of evil, Quinn. We can't use it the same way they can. The magic doesn't work that way."

"We have to check." Quinn looked at Clark, pleading her case. "If it is still there, isn't it better that we grab it and stash it somewhere we can keep it safe and out of their hands?"

Clark stared back at her for several seconds before he gave the barest nod. "It would be nice to deny them access to that particular source of power."

Quinn resisted the urge to clap. She had regretted not finding a way to get the magical gem out of the caverns the last time she was here. Myles Hickman and the others had managed so much evil using it.

Clark locked the car's doors again with a click of the key fob. The car chirped in response. "Let's go see if there's even power for the elevator down there. It might be a moot point if we can't get down to the caverns. Let's hurry up, though. I don't want to be here any longer than we have to."

Clark once again led the way, followed by Miranda and the two eighteen-year-olds. Soon they were making their way down the long basement hallway. Most of the doors lining the corridor stood open. A lot of them had been locked when they'd been here before.

Quinn stole a look inside the room that used to hold all the weapons the last time she was here. That room was cleaned out. Most of the others still held odds and ends, but nothing they found useful enough to take with them. They reached the morgue-like room at the end of the hall. This was where the comatose bodies of the candidates being prepared for possession had been held. The doors on either side of the room were open, giving them easy access to the hallway on the far side.

Quinn couldn't wait any longer. She pushed past Clark and raced ahead to see if the elevator to the caverns below still worked. She beamed a smile back at the flashlights of her companions as the elevator hummed to life when she punched the button.

"Quinn, you need to be careful," Clark admonished her. "You still don't know what you'll find down here. Even though the upper floors were deserted, we don't know what was left down below."

"It's obvious the place is completely deserted at this point, Clark. Can't you feel the emptiness? Plus, there's something else about it. There's nothing, uh, I don't know, nothing wrong with it anymore. It's like it's clean now."

Clark shook his head to disagree but didn't say anything as the elevator doors opened and everyone stepped inside.

When they reached the rocky caverns below, everything was dark. Quinn found an electrical switch on the wall beside the elevator and tried it. To her delight, the string of overhead lights clipped to the ceiling down the long passage turned on, filling the cave with a warm yellow glow. They all put their flashlights away and started down the tunnel.

While there was no wrongness in the building above,

that wasn't the case down here. Quinn's back itched between her shoulder blades as if someone stood behind her watching what she was doing from a hidden place. Her hand moved to her Bowie knife, which was still hanging in its inverted sheath beneath her right arm.

"We should probably check out the cavern," Quinn said, despite the sense of foreboding she felt. When no one answered her, she started down the tunnel.

CHAPTER SIX

The sickly-sweet fetid odor of decay met them about halfway to the cavern.

"What is that?" Taylor asked.

"It's not good," Clark replied.

Miranda nodded. "That's the smell of death."

They neared the opening to the large cavern that had held the pedestal and magical brazier. The acrid odor had grown into something so tangible it could almost be tasted. Quinn's stomach lurched in response. She fought down the burning taste of bile in her throat as she regained control.

Then they reached the entrance and stared into the cavern.

The brazier atop the stone pedestal had been removed. Something else had been left behind, or rather, many somethings, piled all around it.

Taylor gasped and choked back tears. "Oh, my God, no."

Quinn didn't blame for her reaction. The jumble of bloated bodies lying around the pedestal were in various states of decay. Even through the rictus of death, though, she could recognize most of them. They had been her fellow candidates. She'd trained next to most of them at one time or another. They'd all been sent into the VR world created by VirSync to assassinate the company's opponents.

"They killed them, Quinn," Taylor whispered. "They killed all of them as if they were nothing but trash."

A voice sounded from the air around them, coming from nowhere and everywhere at once. "They *were* trash. We had no need for them anymore."

Quinn recognized the voice. She scanned the room, trying to find the source. It was the demon-possessed candidate Jared. She thought she'd killed him during their escape a month ago.

Apparently not.

"Where are you, Jared? Show yourself."

Laughter filled the room and echoed off the walls. "You can't see me. No one can see me. I warned you that you wouldn't be able to be rid of me so easily. I still remain. I still have power over this place."

Miranda sketched a glowing rune in the air with a fingertip, then hissed in response to the spell she'd cast. "It's the spirit of the demon, released when you killed the body it used as an earthly vessel. Either they couldn't assign it to another body or chose not to."

Clark smirked. "My guess is they chose not to. It's just the kind of punishment for failure demonkind likes to use to make an example of one of their own." The hunter looked around the room and raised his voice. "You're a cautionary tale for the next of your ilk who passes by, aren't you? You're a warning. You have no body to inhabit, and you can't return to the netherworld. You're stuck somewhere between."

"So what if I am? That doesn't mean I'm powerless."

Clark laughed. "I'm betting it does. Quinn, you came down here to look for something. Go and search. We'll wait here for you to come back. Hurry up; we need to leave."

Jared had fallen silent. Still, the memory of the disembodied voice creeped Quinn out. She hurried across the cavern and went out through a gap in the far side to a series of caves where she'd hidden the Ruby Heart the last time she was here. After scrambling through the caves and passages, Quinn reached the shallow pool of water where she'd submerged the magical gemstone to hide if from the cultists.

Bending down, Quinn groped around the bottom of the smooth stone basin for the fist-sized ruby. She searched for several minutes until she was drenched from flailing around in the water. It wasn't there. Myles and the others must have found it and taken it with them when they left.

She trudged back to the main cavern, where the others waited amidst the bodies strewn about the stone floor. She shook her head when her companions looked her way. "It's gone. They found it."

Jared's voice cackled with delight. "Of course, they found it. Each of the candidates was tasked with searching. They were all told that only the one who found the gem was worthy of leaving the cavern alive. The others were killed one at a time by my brethren."

Clark shook his head. "Come on, Quinn. There's

nothing more you can do here. Let's leave this creature to his solitary existence."

"Oh, Hunter, there's no leaving this place for you or your companions." Jared's cackling laughter echoed around the cavern.

A groan near Quinn's feet caught her attention. She stifled a scream as the body at her feet jerked to life and rolled over to stare up at her with bulging black eyes.

Miranda shouted, "The demon is using necromantic magic. It's animating the bodies to attack us. Everyone, get out before they all come to life!"

It was too late for that, though. Ten of the corpses started moving, lurching and stumbling as they climbed to their feet. The zombies didn't move very fast, but there were so many of them that there was no way for Quinn and the others to avoid them. That slowed them down long enough for the remainder of the slowly reanimating bodies to reach them.

Clark had pulled out his gleaming silver short sword and started laying about, chopping at the undead around him.

Quinn drew her Bowie knife and turned in time to thrust it into the bloated belly of the reanimated body reaching for her.

A flood of putrid fluid and gas rushed from around her blade, drenching her arm and causing her to retch as she pulled her knife back to stab it in again and again.

The smell was bad enough, but the worst part was, the thing wasn't going down.

"How the hell do I kill these things?"

Across the cavern, much closer to the entrance, Clark called, "Stab 'em in the head or decapitate them."

His enchanted blade sliced downward to hack the top half of a skull away from its body. The undead creature slumped to the ground.

Quinn switched her grip. She drove her knife upward through the bottom of the corpse's chin and into its brain from below.

Just as with Clark's opponent, this one went limp and fell back to the stone floor. Two more had risen just behind it, though. They shuffled forward, reaching for Quinn.

By the entrance, several of the zombie creatures moved toward Miranda. She wove her hands in the air in front of her, and twin bursts of energy lanced outward from her right palm toward the undead. The power of the energy charge knocked the two shambling figures over backward, where they flailed on the ground, trying to get back to their feet.

"There's got to be a way to remove the animation spell," Miranda shouted. "Keep them off me while I try to find out how the spirit is controlling them."

"Easier said than done," Taylor yelled, dodging between two of the roaming corpses. "These things aren't speedy, but there are a lot of them. Plus, they're gross and really smelly."

The tech witch punched one of the creatures as it reached for her. The blow had no visible effect, and the zombie clutched her arm before she could pull it back, tight enough that she couldn't get away.

"Agh, it's got me!"

Quinn kicked another of the animated corpses and

knocked it off balance. It tumbled into two of its brethren, and they fell over. "Hang on, Taylor. I'll be right there."

She charged in the direction of her friend, spinning and twisting to avoid the grasping hands of the zombies reaching for her. The whole time, Jared's cackling filled the room.

One zombie rose directly in front of her and Quinn charged straight at it, bringing her Bowie knife around from the left to plunge into the thing's ear. The blow skewered the skull, with the point coming out the other side.

It fell, but the bone trapped her blade, putting her off-balance as she tried to pull the knife free.

Taylor screamed again.

Quinn snarled and placed her black-booted foot on the reanimated corpse's face while she retrieved her knife with a yank.

It was just enough of a distraction to let another pair of zombies come up behind her and grab Quinn's shoulders as she stood. They pulled her back two steps, each one holding onto an arm and tugging as if trying to tear her in half.

They were stronger than she expected dead people to be. They might be slow, but they didn't lack in the muscle department.

"Hang on, Taylor," Quinn called. "I'm trying to get there."

Clark yelled, "I'll get her. You get to Miranda so she can try to dispel whatever magic is reanimating them."

"Got it." Quinn grunted. It took all her strength to keep her shoulders from being pulled out of their sockets.

Concentrating, Quinn dialed up her stamina bar and

drew on it to enhance her strength. The green bar drained by half, but she sensed the fight's balance shifting.

Using her surging power, Quinn pulled from both sides, slamming the zombies together in front of her. Their heads smacked into each other with an audible crunch, and the bodies fell in a heap to the floor.

Scratch two more zombies.

Quinn searched for the others as she moved toward Miranda.

Clark was true to his word. He had reached Taylor and was cutting down the zombie holding her. He then shoved the girl into the tunnel, where Miranda pressed outward with both palms, holding back four zombies with a sort of forcefield. Their legs moved and pushed, but they made no progress against the witch's invisible barrier.

Taylor darted forward, bending over to scoop up a large stone the size of a frozen chicken. With both hands raising the rock over her head, the girl ran up behind the first of the four zombies facing Miranda's hasty force field. She bashed its skull until it dropped and moved on to the next one in line.

The second zombie turned in place to face her but moved too slowly to stop her from crashing her improvised weapon down on its head. It collapsed in a heap.

By this time, the final two zombies with Miranda turned and noticed the easier target in Taylor. They shambled her way, arms outstretched.

Taylor backpedaled, trying to put some distance between her and the two zombies advancing on her. "Uh, Clark? I think I need you again."

"Can't right now," Clark called. He'd become entangled

with three zombies, who'd closed in on him so he couldn't swing his sword effectively. "Quinn, can you get to her?"

"I've got her." Quinn charged, dodging around two more zombies while reaching for her. She still had her enhanced strength and speed, so getting past them was simple.

Quinn ran up behind the two zombies advancing on Taylor and lowered her shoulder. She slammed into the closest creature from behind, sending it sprawling to the floor. Then she turned to the other one and swung at it, jabbing her Bowie at its head.

Somehow the creature dodged the incoming blow. Her knife missed its head, sliding into the beast's neck instead.

That didn't kill the thing; it only seemed to make it angrier.

Quinn remembered what Clark told her at the beginning of this fight, and she began sawing her blade back and forth while she reached out to grab a handful of greasy black hair.

The zombie leaned toward her, its teeth gnashing, trying to get at her flesh.

Quinn redoubled her efforts and was rewarded when her blade parted the skull from the rest of the body. It collapsed in a pile of twitching limbs.

She turned to Miranda. "What do you need us to do?"

"Just keep them busy enough so they can't get to me while I concentrate on what I sense in the background. I think I can interrupt whatever magic the demon is using to control the bodies."

Quinn nodded and stood beside Taylor, who still had her rock raised and ready to defend the witch.

"Nice choice of a weapon, T."

"Yeah, all I know is Clark is getting me a sword or a pistol or something so I don't have to wait for someone else to come and rescue me. This damsel-in-distress crap is not for me."

More of the zombies began to reanimate. "Hey, Miranda, is it possible that Jared can only control a few of these things at a time?"

"That makes sense, especially since he's in spirit form. We need to do something to distract him so he can't jump from body to body and get them to move."

Quinn noticed a chill against her chest as she stared at the latest of the animated corpses rising to its feet. A sort of hazy film hung around it that drifted away as soon as the zombie was on its feet. The nearly transparent blob floated over to another body, and that one started to move.

"I can see him," Quinn hissed to Miranda and Taylor. "My amulet is enabling me to see him move around and create the zombies."

"We have to stop him from reanimating any more of them," Miranda declared. "I can stop him if we can pin him in one place."

Quinn reached up and pressed the silver oval of her hunter amulet to her chest. The icy-cold of the magical charm burned her skin, but she ignored it. She scanned the room, focusing on following the thing she was now sure had to be the demonic spirit that had formerly inhabited Jared.

As it floated around the room bringing more corpses to life, Quinn noticed it never flew too close to the stone pedestal in the center. In fact, the short stone column had a sort of hazy power of its own when she stared at it while concentrating with her amulet. When Jared floated closer, tendrils laced out from the pedestal in his direction.

"I have an idea, Miranda. Get ready with your trapping spell or whatever. I think we can somehow tie the demon's spirit to the residual magic in the pedestal."

"Good plan," Miranda said. "Can you get him close enough? I can seal him to the magic there if you can."

Quinn nodded and focused on her amulet while she moved toward the pedestal. She had to dodge zombies on the way, and as she neared the rock formation, finishing off the final one standing in her way, magical tendrils laced out in her direction. Instead of shying from them, Quinn welcomed them, using her amulet to grab them.

At first, the tendrils resisted, feeling to Quinn as if she were stretching intangible rubber bands with her mind. She walked closer while she tried to solidify her hold on the magic there.

"Quinn," Miranda called. "What are you doing? The things are coming closer to you."

"Trying out an idea. I don't think they'll come all the way to the pedestal. Jared's afraid of it, aren't you, Jared?"

The voice filling the cavern cackled and said, "I'm not afraid of anything on this plane, Huntress. You, on the other hand, will learn to be afraid of much."

"I don't think so. In fact, Jared, I'm going to sit here and dare you to send your undead minions after me."

To punctuate her claim, Quinn reached the pedestal and hopped up to sit on the flat top. Her legs dangled over the side. She kicked them playfully and laughed, saying, "Come and get me if you can."

Clark, who'd dispatched the zombies attacking him, started her way. "Quinn, what are you playing at? You've gotten yourself surrounded."

"I don't think so. I think Jared is the one who's in trouble, not me."

"Foolish girl," the spirit called. He let out another maniacal laugh. "There's nowhere in here my friends can't get to you."

"Well, here I am." Quinn held her Bowie in front of her, dangling it over the stone floor with her thumb and forefinger. She let it go to clatter on the rocks at the base of the pedestal. "Oh, no, whatever shall I do? I dropped my magic knife."

"Quinn!" Clark shouted.

She held up a hand to stop him while she concentrated on Jared's location. The amorphous blob floated closer to the center of the cavern. Quinn felt the pedestal's tendrils pulling to break free of the hold she had over them and reaching for the spirit blob. She pulled harder with her amulet, bringing them back near the pedestal. She needed him to come closer. Just a bit.

"I'm bored, Jared. You talk a big game, but you're nothing but a loud, annoying ghost. I think you're stuck here and can't go back to the netherworld where you belong. I think Clark's right. You're being punished."

The demon voice snarled, "You have no concept of what I'm capable of, girl."

The blob drifted closer as it circled her. She had to keep him talking.

"So educate me. What's a big, bad demon like you doing stuck down here with a bunch of dead humans? You practically laughed when I killed Jared and freed you. You said I couldn't stop you that easily."

"And I was right." The blob pulsed, taking on a sickly, translucent white appearance instead of remaining transparent. "You *can't* stop me. I'll prove it to you, then make you one of my pets, just like these others."

The two zombies closest to her lurched at Quinn but stopped about five feet from the base of the pedestal.

Quinn grinned. "Is that the best you can do? Just the two of them? They can't even get all the way to me. You're all talk and no action."

Jared snarled, filling the cavern with the buzzing of a million insects. The other newly animated corpses, six in all, shuffled toward the pedestal to join the other two. They also stopped short of reaching Quinn.

A chill ran down her spine. Clark glared at her from across the cavern, and she could feel Taylor's and Miranda's eyes on her back, too. A trickle of sweat dripped down her face, but she resisted wiping it away. It might tip off the spirit about how nervous she was with her plan and how much strain it was to hold onto the pedestal's magic tendrils. That would be bad.

She had to end this before the demon called her bluff.

Quinn pulled her feet up and placed her heels on the edge of the pedestal, then balanced as she stood up, raising her hands over her head.

"I'm tired of your crap, Jared or whoever you are. You're just a powerless crybaby trying to scare us. Maybe we'll stick around and play with you for a little while."

Quinn brought one hand down and pressed her palm

against the amulet, embracing the biting cold of the silver while she waited. A little bit longer, and...

The blob that was the demon spirit drifted closer and pressed against the backs of the nearest zombies, forcing them closer to the pedestal. With each step, Quinn gauged their progress against the potential reach of the magical tendrils she kept under the control of her iron will.

Almost there.

Almost there.

Now!

Quinn released the pedestal's magic.

The intangible tendrils of magic snapped out as if fired from a slingshot, flinging themselves past the zombies to clutch the milky white blob.

"Nooooo!" The voice echoed through the cavern. The blob turned darker, almost black now as the tendrils wrapped around it and drew it closer.

Quinn hopped down and stepped back from the short column of rock. The zombies were frozen in place now. She passed the circle of undead as the tendrils drew the blob all the way back to rest atop the stone outcropping. The pedestal's magic pulsed in tempo with the now-screamed protestations of the demon. The zombies still standing dropped to the floor, whatever magic that had reanimated them now cut off.

"You tricked me, girl. I will get you for this."

Quinn laughed. "How? I trapped you and cut off your power. You can't hurt anyone now."

The voice choked and gasped, and the bubble of energy over the pedestal shrank as the translucent tendrils squeezed it to the flat surface of the stand.

"I know...because you'll be back. I know something you need."

Quinn started to ask about what the demon knew but stopped as the voice screeched. Everyone covered their ears, and then the bubble, the tendrils, and everything magical she'd seen shrank down to nothing and disappeared.

She spun to look at Clark. "What? What does it think I need?"

Clark shook his head. "Don't listen to it. It's a demon. Its power is built on lies."

Quinn glanced back at the now-empty pedestal. The cackling that had filled the room for the last ten minutes was gone, leaving an eerie silence. She shook her head and walked over to where the others stood by the tunnel entrance.

Clark gestured to the corridor with the tip of his sword. "We need to get going. The car is still sitting up there, and the company might still have security patrols come by to check on this place."

Quinn nodded and followed Miranda. Taylor and Clark brought up the rear.

"I'm still holding out to get my own sword, Clark," Taylor said. "You must have a stash around somewhere back at home. I want to take a look."

"You don't need a sword, Taylor. We protected you just fine."

"This time. What about the next time when you all aren't around. I'm an independent and powerful woman, just like Quinn. I deserve a weapon."

"I'll take it under advisement."

"Don't you patronize me!"

Quinn smiled as Taylor went off on a feminist rant.

Clark glanced over his shoulder at Quinn and scowled when he saw the grin on her face. She knew Clark saw her, and she didn't care. Sure, it would mean extra-hard training, but right now, it was so worth it.

It almost took her mind off what demon-Jared's voice had said. What did it know?

CHAPTER SEVEN

Back at the farmhouse, Quinn stared at the water-stained ceiling as she lay in bed. Another night of restless sleep. Two days had passed since the desperate battle in the cavern. She couldn't stop thinking about the final words demon-Jared had said before he was swallowed by whatever inhabited the pedestal.

What had he meant?

A corner of her mind wanted to talk to Clark about it, but she pushed the idea away. He'd only repeat what he'd said in the cavern and tell her it was a taunt and nothing more. She didn't need him using it against her as some sort of training lesson in dealing with evil spirits. She'd be fine on her own in that department, at least for now.

Besides, the team had more on their minds now that they'd discovered VirSync's mysterious disappearance. They'd all tried to come up with a reason for the company's relocation—or perhaps dissolution.

Quinn's stomach growled, and she rolled over and sat up. Her feet hung over the side of the bed as she ran her fingers through her hair, scratching an itch behind her ear as she tried to wake up. The murmur of voices downstairs told her at least two of the others were already awake.

Pulling on a pair of sweatpants, Quinn padded in bare feet into the hallway and down the stairs to the main floor. The cold wooden floorboards reminded her it was getting into the fall season. The house didn't have any heat since the fuel oil tank had been emptied by the previous owners before they moved out. Getting a company to come out and fill it would draw unwanted attention to the fact they were squatting there.

Before it got too cold, they'd have to move to somewhere with more than just a well and hijacked electric.

Quinn entered the kitchen and headed straight for the smell of coffee.

Taylor and Miranda chatted over their breakfast. Both looked up as she entered.

"Hey, Quinn," Taylor said. "Girl, you look like crap. You know that?"

Miranda shushed Taylor and smiled at Quinn. "Still having trouble sleeping?"

"Yeah, but I'll be all right. I think I just need to get back in a groove and into a routine." Quinn poured some coffee into a mug and dropped in three spoonfuls of sugar, stirring as she stared out the kitchen window at the farmyard. Clark's car wasn't parked in its usual spot. "He's up and out early. Where'd he go this time? He's barely been around."

Taylor chuckled. "I'm surprised you're complaining. If he *was* here, he'd be working you to the bone on training routines down in the cellar."

Miranda laughed. "She's not wrong, Quinn. You can't have it both ways."

"Where did he go?"

Miranda replied, "He was leaving when I came down this morning. He said he needed to follow up with an informant who might know what VirSync is up to."

Quinn walked to the table and sat down.

Taylor slid a clean bowl and a box of cereal over. "Here. Eat something. You'll feel better with some food in you."

Quinn filled the bowl and poured some milk from the carton. "What's on the agenda for you two today?"

"I'm almost ready to start testing the new computer system with Miranda," Taylor said. "I've got a crude VR headset worked out, so we just need to make sure the software is loaded properly alongside the magical code to make it all work. Once that's finished, we can get you into the VR world. Then it's up to you to figure out what you need to do next."

"Yeah, like I have a clue about that," Quinn muttered around a mouthful of cereal.

Miranda asked, "How did you do it before? You gained the skills you have somehow."

"I don't know. I just sort of guessed they were there, and they were. You know, like in a new video game where you learn what all the buttons in the interface do a little at a time. I would comment aloud that I wanted to go faster, and the stamina boost thing showed up."

"Well," Miranda said, "There you go. Treat it like a game and try out some of the things you can do in a game but not in the real world. See if they pop up inside the VR system."

"I guess so. Of course, first, you need to get the thing up and running and make sure it doesn't melt my brain or something."

Taylor shrugged. "Like I said. We're close. Miranda has the spell work dialed in…"

"I said I think I have it dialed in. There's a difference."

Taylor nodded in Miranda's direction. "What she said. Anyway, my guess is you'll be ready to get in there soon."

"I know Clark is tracking down leads on his end, but you haven't had any luck on your end tracking VirSync down, T?" Quinn asked.

"Miranda and I were chatting about that when you came down. It's weird for any company to just up and move like that. There are no news stories about it, even locally. I've got a search bot looking for any sign of them. It'll alert me if anything pops up on the news sites."

Miranda pressed her lips together and shook her head. "VirSync was a popular gaming company, but they weren't that large, compared to other Baltimore-area businesses. That could explain why no one noticed. Also, no one in a position to report it might know they've moved."

"Where did they go, though?" Quinn asked. "It's been two days since we found out. Could they have moved to another state?"

"Clark says no," Miranda said. "He thinks they just went underground. They picked this location to hatch their plans for a reason. There must be something here they need or were preparing for. I agree with him. There's a reason they're here in Baltimore."

Quinn gestured with her spoon after a few seconds of thinking and said, "What could they be doing? They killed all the remaining candidates. There isn't training going on anymore unless they've got another group of candidates somewhere."

"That's not a bad idea, Quinn," Taylor said. "What if they're recruiting more slayers for their system? If they are, I might be able to track them down that way."

"How?" Quinn asked.

"You both can help me. I think we can use a magical component in the search if I understand some of what Miranda explained about how her magic works."

Miranda shrugged. "If it means I don't have to memorize lines of computer code for a while, I'm in."

Taylor stood and started clearing the breakfast dishes. "Let's clean this up and then we can get started."

Quinn picked up her cereal bowl and drank down the rest of the milk and soggy cereal in it then stood to take it to the sink. On the way back, she grabbed her half-finished coffee and followed the other two into the dining room.

Taylor sat down behind the computer workstation she'd set up at the end of the dining room table. She tapped a few commands into a wireless keyboard and then leaned back in the ladder-back chair and crossed her legs so she could type on the keyboard as it sat in her lap.

On the table in front of her sat a row of three monitors. As Taylor tapped, Quinn and Miranda moved around to stand behind her and watch the screens.

The one on the left made no sense to Quinn. Random characters and numbers scrolled by at a speed that seemed impossible to read. Taylor seemed to be able to parse it, though, because as she stared at the code, she nodded and typed in new information, which caused the lines on the screen to scroll even faster.

"What's all that mean?" Quinn asked.

"It's the programming language they used to write the code at VirSync."

"You taught yourself a new programming language in what, a few weeks?"

"It wasn't hard."

Quinn laughed. Taylor always downplayed her abilities. This was just another one of those times.

Miranda didn't let it drop, though. "That is precisely why Clark's calling you our tech witch is more than just a clever turn of phrase. It's destiny."

When both Quinn and Taylor turned to answer her words with blank stares, Miranda pressed onward. "Ladies, none of this is an accident. There's no such thing, really. There are forces at work here to restore balance in the universe."

"But Clark said..." Quinn began.

"Clark said what? That Earth is the battleground between good and evil?"

"Something like that."

"Well, he's biased, and I believe he's wrong."

Quinn shook her head. "You were there two days ago when we fought a disembodied demon and a horde of zombies, right?"

"I'm not saying evil doesn't exist. Believe me, it does, and what VirSync did was evil with a capital E, but this isn't only about good versus evil. That will always be there. This is about the Balance."

"Balance?" Taylor asked. "What does that even mean?"

"No, not 'balance.' *The* Balance. The thing that keeps the whole universe from simultaneously imploding and exploding when antimatter and matter mix without some sort of stabilizer."

"So, I'm…we're that stabilizer?" Quinn asked.

"In a way," Miranda said. "But it's more than that. This was what my coven was working on when you and the other slayers started hunting us. Remember the city councilman who was killed in your first VR trip? It was that upset in the Balance he called us here to study."

"I thought you were working with Clark."

"Quinn, you were there when I was forced to start working with Clark, but that doesn't mean I'm working *for* Clark. I'm working alongside him."

"Does he know that?" Taylor asked. "Because I'm pretty sure he's under the assumption that he's in charge. He *is* the last living hunter, after all."

"That's the point, I think," Miranda explained. "This is a course correction by the universe before something bad happens."

"The universe, really?" Quinn asked. This was too metaphysical for her.

"Yes. It's Nature, or Gaia, or whatever you want to call it. Many of us believe it's not the battle between light and dark that keeps us safe, it's the Balance—the natural checks against one side being more powerful than the other. Twenty years ago, the purges began. Before anyone knew it, the hunters, who were the protectors of everyone against the forces of Evil with a capital E, were gone. I remember my parents worrying about it. They feared that with the hunters out of the picture, the netherworlders would take over the next day."

Quinn nodded. "I wondered about that when Clark first told me about it. If I was them, I would have swooped in and filled the void. But they didn't."

"Because some humans and supernaturals of all sorts saw the danger. They worked together to stem the tide, at least for a time." Miranda pointed to Quinn. "But now you're here. A month ago, you declared a new sort of hunter clan, one composed not just of hunters, but of other supernaturals, and even mundanes. That may be the key to staving off the advent of a new dark age the world hasn't seen for over a thousand years."

Taylor scowled and said, "Who's the 'mundane?' Me? I prefer 'tech witch' if you don't mind. That word is so…"

"Mundane?" Quinn quipped, then laughed. "We appreciate you, I promise. You deserve a better title to describe your place on our team."

Taylor smiled and turned to look at Miranda.

"Hey, I meant no offense. It's what we call non-magical people. You have demonstrated you're way more capable than most humans would be."

"So what does this have to do with Clark? Does it mean he's wrong in what he's doing?" Quinn asked. "He doesn't want this new dark age you're warning us about any more than you do."

Miranda shook her head. "No, he's working toward the same purpose, although he's on a parallel path. I only wanted to point out that his way isn't the only way. I like what he's done so far. He's shown he's flexible with the way he's training you. I think he understands a change is afoot; that something new is coming, at least deep down."

"So," Quinn began, "we're here to represent nature's new counter to a resurgence of evil, manifesting now using magic and technology together. We just have to find out where they are. They took the VR rigs with them. We have to assume they are going to use them again to send out more slayers."

Taylor snapped her fingers. "Maybe we should have started looking at that from the beginning."

Quinn raised an eyebrow in question.

"Think about it, Quinn. If they're still using the VR rigs to assassinate people or commit other crimes, that means they have to be connected to the web somehow. I'm convinced they're using the interconnectivity of every-thing electronic to help transmit them to their target's vicinity, so we might be able to track them down."

When neither Quinn or Miranda said anything, Taylor reached over and picked up the crude VR headset on which she'd been working. "This uses the scrapped tech we recovered from the VirSync storerooms. It came from the same source as their existing tech. That means they use related components. All I have to do is figure out which ones and I should be able to localize their presence when they're plugged in."

Miranda waited a few seconds, then she said, "What are you waiting for? Start searching."

"Uh, yeah," Taylor said. "The bad news is, I have to wait until they're using the VR system again. Until then, there won't be anything to detect."

Quinn nodded. "So we need to draw them out. That shouldn't be too hard."

Clark's voice came from behind them. "Draw who out?"

Quinn spun, startled. Clark always came and went in silence. She said, "The slayers. Taylor thinks she can find the new VirSync location but needs to wait until they're using the VR tech again. That means we need to set up a trap for them. Unless you found them while you were gone this morning?"

Clark shook his head. "No, I had to meet with someone I'd offered protection to over the years. They laid low after the other attacks happened, but they need to come out of hiding to prepare for an upcoming event that's happening soon."

Clark's brow furrowed with worry as he said it, something Quinn didn't miss. "And you're not happy with that decision. What's the big deal, maybe we can use this to lay our trap for the slayers."

"We may not have to," Clark said. "I think this is what they were working for the whole time. I can't believe I didn't see it before."

"What is this big event, Clark?" Miranda asked. "I don't remember hearing about anything supernatural happening soon."

"You wouldn't have heard about this. It was kept on a strict need-to-know basis. There's going to be a major fae summit held here in Baltimore in a week or so. I thought it would have been called off given the attacks in the area. Apparently, I was wrong."

"A fae summit," Miranda said. "With all the fae leaders in one place?"

Clark nodded.

"If Myles and the demons he's working with succeed in taking out the fae leadership," Miranda mused, "it would leave a huge void in the supernatural world. It would be nearly impossible to recover from a blow like that. The fae would retreat from the world again, taking their magic with them. The void would allow the netherworlders to enter and fill that space. The last time that happened was after the fall of the Roman Empire. The Dark Ages acquired that name for a reason."

Now that it had been explained to her, Quinn knew what Miranda meant. "We have to stop them, Clark, and that means I need to train harder and work on a way to counter them on their own turf. We have to get the VR rig up and running and find out where VirSync is operating sooner rather than later."

"The tech witch is on it," Taylor said, grinning. "I can multitask with the best of them. If they turn their system on again, I'll know it. I'll make sure your rig is ready to go when we need it."

Quinn hoped Taylor was right because right now, the hacker held their only hope of finding and countering VirSync before the summit.

CHAPTER EIGHT

It was two more days before Taylor picked up a ping on her searches for technology related to the discarded VirSync gear they'd found in the storeroom. She announced her success with a loud whoop from the dining room, followed by a shouted, "Got 'em!"

Quinn and Clark were in the basement training when they heard Taylor's shout. Quinn rose from the mat, rubbing her shoulder and happy for a break in the current drill. She'd started to get better and even managed to get past Clark's formidable defenses on a few occasions. Still, those small victories were few and far between.

Clark tossed her a towel from the peg by the stairs. "That sounds promising. I was beginning to think her claims were all hype."

"I never doubted her, though I was getting anxious that she might be trying to do too much. She's barely gotten any sleep in forty-eight hours."

"Let's see what she's discovered."

Clark started up the stairs with Quinn right behind him.

Miranda stood behind Taylor when the pair arrived, leaning over her back, staring at the center screen arrayed in front of her. She pointed at the center screen. "What's that?"

Taylor beamed. "That is a ping from a tracking bot I created. It found a nearly identical electronic serial number to one of the components in the VR rig I created. Someone fired it up for about five minutes yesterday, then shut it back down. I can't tell you exactly when. My bot is just reading device logs on local servers. I'd need to be a lot closer to the network they're on to be able to track it in real-time, but I know the area it came from."

Clark walked over to join Miranda behind Taylor. Quinn followed.

The hunter pointed at the blinking dot on the map on the screen to the right. "That's in the middle of downtown. There are dozens of places they could be hiding there. Can you localize it?"

"Maybe." Taylor's fingers tapped on the keyboard, and the map zoomed in to an area just a few city blocks wide. The pulsing red circle now filled the whole display. A few seconds after zooming in, though, the red ring began to shrink, and finally, it hovered over a single building.

Taylor tapped the screen. "That's where they are."

Clark shook his head. "That building has to be at least twenty stories tall. There have to be more than a dozen businesses in there."

Taylor frowned, probably because she'd expected congratulations. "I can narrow it down for you a little.

They'd need a pretty large broadband connection to handle what they're doing, especially if they're planning on sending out more than one slayer at a time."

She tapped a few more commands in and glanced at the first screen where a standard web search window had opened. She clicked on one of the results before Quinn could read it, and soon two windows opened. They each showed some sort of online control panel.

"What's that?" Quinn asked.

"I'm in both the phone and cable company's maintenance systems. They should tell me which accounts in that building are using the most data in, and more importantly, out."

"And?" Clark asked.

"There are three companies using the kind of bandwidth I'd expect to see from the VirSync VR system." Taylor studied the list that popped up. After scanning the screen for a few seconds, she pointed at the first company listed. "This one is a media advertising firm that probably uploads large video files on a regular basis for clients. They'd use a lot of bandwidth. The next one is a cyber-security firm. They also need a big pipe to move tons of data."

Her finger tapped the last entry on the list. "This has to be it. What does a small brokerage firm need all that raw cyber power for? They deal in stock trades that consist of small packets of data. Sure, there are a lot of them, but there's no way that accounts for this kind of usage. Plus, there's been a spike in data in the last few weeks. If I'm right, that's the one."

Quinn leaned forward. "Handon Services, LLC. I've never heard of them."

"Me either," Miranda replied. "It sort of makes them a great cover. Maybe Myles Hickman and the cult behind VirSync created shell companies to move to when needed. They'd be a perfect way to provide cover for what they're doing."

"We have to scout them to be sure," Clark said. "I'll go tonight."

"I'm going, too," Quinn interjected.

Clark started to shake his head, then stopped himself. "Fine, but listen to me and do as I say. This is a recon mission. We just need to verify they're there. Once that's done, we can decide what to do next."

"Why don't we attack while we're there?" Quinn asked.

"Because there are only two of us. We have no idea how many people they have there to protect their operation. If it's them, we need to even the odds before we confront them directly. It'll be risky enough to expose the fact that we're on to their location. It might just make them bug out again. Then we'd be back to square one."

Quinn's shoulders sagged with disappointment. She wanted to get some payback from the people who'd killed all the candidates and left their bodies to rot back in that cavern.

"Quinn, go get a shower and some rest. We're not leaving until nearly midnight. I want you fresh and with your wits about you tonight."

Quinn nodded and headed for the bathroom upstairs. Her mind drifted back to what had happened in the cavern, and she wondered what new part of the cult's evil plot await their arrival tonight. She'd find out soon enough.

When she woke up from her nap hours after dark, it surprised her. Clark's incessant drills and training regimen had clearly taken a lot out of her. Her excitement about their mission, coupled with feeling refreshed from the shower and nap, bounced her out of bed to get dressed.

When she came downstairs to get something to eat, it took her a few seconds to locate everyone.

Taylor spotted her first, her head popping up from behind the trio of computer monitors in the dining room. "Hey, Clark went out earlier and picked up pizza. It's in the fridge."

"Cool, I'm starving. Anything new on tonight's target?"

"Nope. I've tried to find out more about what the brokerage company does, but there isn't much information out there about them or the people who work there."

Quinn nodded and glanced into the next room. Clark sat on the old sofa there in the den. He had his sword out and ran a stone across the blade in slow even strokes, sharpening an edge that was probably already as sharp as it ever needed to be.

"Can't that thing already split a hair if needed?"

Clark looked up and smiled. "Of course, but maintaining the tools of your trade is never a bad idea. You should sharpen your Bowie, too. Sit down. I'll show you how to do it."

"I need to get something to eat. I'll be right back."

"Go ahead," Clark said. "I'll move in there to the table while you heat something up."

Quinn returned to the kitchen and got herself a few

slices of pizza. She popped them in the microwave and went down to the basement, where Clark kept their small stash of edged weapons. She retrieved her knife and returned to the kitchen just in time to get her hot pizza from the microwave.

She sat down, setting the Bowie knife in its sheath beside her plate. She picked up a slice of pizza, folded it in half New York-style, and started in on it. It was delicious.

Between bites, she slid the knife in Clark's direction.

He laughed and pushed it back to her. "I'm not sharpening it for you. It's not my blade. Finish your dinner, and I'll show you what to do. This is as important as all the training we've done downstairs. I should have started you on it sooner, but I got distracted by trying to break through the barrier that kept you from progressing."

Quinn wolfed down the remaining pizza and took the dish to the sink before returning to the table. Clark had laid a sharpening stone identical to his on the table next to her sheathed knife. It was about eight inches long and two inches wide.

He also took a small plastic squeeze bottle with a narrow conical tip from the bag on the floor beside his chair. He squirted a small dot of liquid on Quinn's stone and capped the bottle.

"What's that?"

"Honing oil," Clark replied. "It helps lubricate the blade as you work on the edge. Now take out your knife and move the stone over in front of you."

Quinn pulled the Bowie from the sheath and reached for the stone to pick it up.

"No, leave the stone on the table. Just slide it over in front of you with the narrow side closest to you."

"You picked yours up," Quinn argued.

"Yes, but my blade is longer than yours. Leaving the stone on the table will help you maintain the proper angle for an optimal edge. I'll put mine down to show you what I mean."

Quinn watched as Clark demonstrated what he wanted her to do. Soon she pushed the blade across the stone in long smooth motions, concentrating on keeping the edge at the right angle. As she did, she saw a sort of silver glow around the point where the knife met the stone.

"Hey, there's some sort of... I don't know, like a light coming from the knife."

Clark smiled. "That's good. I wasn't sure if you would see anything or not. It tells me that we don't have to rely on the VR for all your training. A hunter's blade is important. It's almost a physical extension of you. What you're seeing is the blade's blessed magic sort of telling you the best angle and speed to use to get the perfect edge."

Quinn focused on the faint light coming from her blade and tried to keep it constant as she moved the edge over the stone. She noticed that tiny shifts in her angle of attack caused the light to dim or brighten based on what she did. She started working on getting the brightest, most consistent glow she could from the blade as she worked.

Across the table from her, Clark nodded. He picked up his stone and returned to working on his sword.

When Taylor came in sometime later, Quinn had no idea how long she'd been sitting there with the stone and blade. She'd reached some sort of Zen state working the edge of her knife. She barely looked up at her friend to acknowledge her presence. If she took her eyes off the Bowie, the glow faded.

"I wondered what the two of you were up to in here. All I could hear was that strange scraping sound. Now I see you both in some sort of trance over your sharp and pointy things."

Quinn sighed and lifted her blade up from the stone. She put the knife down beside the sheath and raised her hands over her head to stretch. "It is kind of relaxing to sit here and do this, I'm not going to lie."

"That reminds me," Taylor said, turning to Clark. "When do I get my sword. I'm thinking something like the one the Witcher carries strapped to his back."

"First, no one carries a sword that way. There's no way you can draw a long-bladed weapon from its sheath when it's on your back without bending the blade. The angle doesn't work."

"And second?"

"Second, no, you don't get a sword."

"Why not? I need to be able to defend myself. Remember what happened in the cavern?"

"You're not a hunter. A sword is a hunter's weapon."

"Quinn's a hunter, and she doesn't have a sword," Taylor countered.

"Quinn chose her blade when she went through training at VirSync. It seems to have imprinted on her. I've tried sword drills with her, but it hasn't taken yet. It might be something she has to learn once you get that VR rig working."

"All right, so no sword. How about a big shiny knife like hers? It's not a sword, so I can have one, right?"

Clark stifled a low groan, which brought a smile to Quinn's face. Taylor could be a force of nature when she wanted something.

"Fine. You want a knife, try this." Clark reached into his ever-present leather jacket and unclipped something. He pulled it out and tossed it in Taylor's direction.

The girl caught it and held it up. It was a narrow-bladed knife in a leather sheath five or maybe six total inches long. The metal from the blade stretched back and became a rounded handle. There were quarter-inch holes bored in the exposed steel. Quinn had never seen a knife like it.

"What the hell is this tiny thing? This will be next to useless in a fight."

"It's not useless. It's a throwing knife. You have no business getting close enough to use a real knife. Learn to use that, and I'll get you a few more like it. There's a target set up on the wall downstairs."

Taylor drew the shiny steel knife from its sheath and brandished it. "A throwing knife; that's pretty cool. I need to go look up videos on how to use one."

The girl left the room to get back on her computer, and Clark sighed. A satisfied smile crossed his face. "I thought she'd ask me to train her to use it."

Quinn chuckled. "You should be glad she has the internet to learn from."

"Believe me, I am." Clark glanced at his watch and slid his chair back from the table. "It's time to leave. We want to be down there just after midnight. Hopefully, any guards will be good and bored by then."

Quinn glanced at the clock on the wall in the corner. Her eyebrows shot up. "Wow, I didn't realize it was so late."

"Time flies when you're having fun."

Quinn sheathed her knife and then handed the stone back to Clark.

He shook his head. "No, you keep it. Use it to work at your blade when you have the time. I think it will help you bond with your hunter side."

"Hunt*ress*," Quinn corrected.

"Uh, yeah, that's what I meant."

Quinn knew he wasn't buying into her whole huntress meme, but it felt right to her, so she was going to keep using it. She attached the sheathed Bowie knife to the shoulder holster rig she'd been using and slipped her arms through the straps. She retrieved her black leather jacket and pulled it on, concealing the knife beneath it.

Clark had returned his sword to its hidden sheath beneath his knee-length coat, then turned to Quinn. "Ready?"

She nodded, and the two of them left the farmhouse to head downtown.

CHAPTER NINE

Clark left his car several blocks from the target building, pulling into a garage and parking on the second floor.

When Quinn checked her phone against the address, she asked, "Why aren't we getting closer? Are you afraid they might see us coming? This beat-up old car doesn't exactly scream, 'Hunters are coming,' you know."

"This location offers us quick access to several quick ways out of the city if we're followed on the way back."

"Yeah, but we're like two or three blocks away. That's a long way to run if they're chasing us."

"Don't worry, we're hunters. We do the chasing."

Quinn hoped Clark's bravado wasn't misplaced. She wasn't afraid of anything catching her. She knew how fast she could go, especially with her ability to boost things. She wondered how Clark would do with his perpetual limp. He did fine during training, ignoring whatever pained him during their bouts, but she'd never seen him run anywhere.

"Quinn, keep yourself focused. Let's get moving."

She realized she still sat in the car, and Clark stood by the passenger door waiting for her. "Sorry, just going over a mental checklist of what we might need if we have to get out of here quickly."

Clark nodded. "It's good to have contingency plans, but you can't let yourself get distracted so badly that you don't pay attention to what's around you."

"Got it. Keep my mind in the game. I'm good."

"Great. Let's go."

Clark headed to the stairs that led to the street level. Before following him, Quinn noted they were on the second level and marked the car's location.

On the street, they headed north one block and then turned left and started west. The building was one of many similar tall concrete-and-glass office buildings in this part of the city.

As they drew closer to the target, Quinn asked, "Do you think we should mask our presence or something? We've got that hide-in-the-shadows thing we can do."

"No, first we'll just walk on by like we're on our way home after a late drink at a nearby bar. I want to see what they have in place in the way of security first, and the front of the building is too well-lit to make our shadow-hiding abilities fool-proof. Once I've got a good idea what we're up against, we'll check around back where it's darker and we can hide."

"Won't they see us if we walk by in plain sight?"

"Of course, but that's the point. Who'd suspect us as anything but a couple of late-night pedestrians coming home from a club?"

"No one, I guess." Quinn understood the logic of it, but her stomach churned with worry as they passed the address Taylor had given them. Quinn tried to act nonchalant as she walked beside Clark.

She worked to take in as much as possible. That included counting the visible video cameras both outside the building and inside the glassed-in first-floor lobby. It presented a challenge to look without seeming to be doing so, so she turned her head and smiled as if she were looking at Clark while she looked past him at the lobby.

Two, no, three guards stood inside the well-lit area. The third one was partially hidden back by the elevator. Even masked in the shadows, there was no way they'd make it past all three guards.

As they neared the corner after the building, Quinn whispered, "That's a lot of guards to be up this late, don't you think?"

"Not really. They could be the only ones for the whole building and are just checking in at the lobby. It might just be a coincidence. Turn left. We'll circle the block and see if there's another entrance."

Quinn did as she was told. To play out the masquerade, she hooked her arm in the crook of Clark's elbow. She figured if they really were returning from a bar, it would look more realistic. She didn't play for that team, but the bad guys didn't know that.

"Nice touch," Clark muttered as he brought up his free hand and patted hers where it rested on his forearm.

"Just trying to make sure we don't get spotted. Don't let it go to your head."

"No chance of that, kid. You're way too young for me."

Quinn nodded at the sidewalk ahead. "The streetlight is out up there. We could shift into shadow mode and try to access the rear of the building. There might be a loading dock down the alley on the left."

"Good call. Move left to walk up beside the building. Try to shift into the shadows slowly as you enter the dark area so you sort of fade from sight if anyone is watching. They'll think it's too dark here for the camera to penetrate. I'll be right behind you."

Quinn nodded and pulled her arm free to walk closer to the building. She focused on her amulet and tried to meld with the shadows the way she had before. She murmured as she walked, "Mist."

It took a few seconds longer than she'd planned, but it eventually worked, and soon she turned the corner into the alley with the familiar haze surrounding her visual field. She waited for Clark, invisible and unnoticeable as long as she didn't attack anyone or do anything overt to draw attention.

She looked around for Clark. He should have been here by now.

His voice came from directly behind her. "Forget I'd be hidden too?"

Quinn jumped, and she turned to look for the source of the voice. She could sort of make out the hazy outline of a figure standing in front of her. "Uh, yeah, I did. I've never seen it from the other side before, just when I did it."

A low chuckle emerged from the darkness. "Come on. Let's see what things look like back here. Hopefully, we can find a way to get in this way. It might also make a good exit point for when we make the real infiltration."

Quinn started to nod, then stopped. He couldn't see her. "I'm right behind you, or I'll try to be as long as I can sort of see you."

"You can see me?"

"Yes, you're sort of a hazy Clark-shaped outline in the dark."

"Good. It takes some people a long time to be able to locate a magically hidden person. Some never get the hang of it. Stay close and keep your eyes open. Remember, the more light, the easier it is for someone to notice you, even masked. The shadow-hiding isn't perfect."

Clark's form shifted forward, and Quinn moved to follow him down the alley to the loading dock at the rear of the building.

As they neared the pool of bright light around the rear entrance, Quinn counted three cameras, two focused up and down the alley approaches. The last was angled to pick up the immediate area around the dock. There were no guards in sight. There was a faint musky odor in the air that was sort of weird, but other than that, she couldn't sense anything.

"Damn," Clark hissed.

"What?" Quinn whispered.

"Shifters. Somewhere near. I can smell them."

"That musky smell? I can smell it, too."

"Good, that's something else I don't have to teach you. I was hoping you got that inside the VR game on your first hunt."

He might be right. Her first target as a slayer for VirSync had been a shifter.

She tapped Clark on the shoulder as he started to move forward, causing him to stop.

"What is it?"

"I thought the shifters were on our side nowadays? You said all the supernaturals now secretly worked with the humans of the world."

"Most of them are, but they're people just like us, so they can take sides. Some are motivated by the same greed and desires as anyone else."

Quinn drew in a deep breath through her nose to see if she could sense how close the werewolves, or whatever shifter type they faced, were. The odor hadn't changed in intensity, but she didn't know if that was because of proximity or something else. She had no way of knowing how far away she had to be to detect one.

Clark whispered, "I'll head by the dock first and take up a position on the far side to check around there. Once I'm in place, you head up and check the area around the door. Move slowly as you enter the light. It'll help the masking magic work. A bored night guard probably won't notice you. See if it's unlocked, or if you can spot any guards around inside, then move away back to the shadows."

"Got it. Be careful."

"You, too."

The vague form ahead of her moved around to the other side of the alley and then passed the loading dock area. It stayed far away from the lights by the big double doors leading inside. The farther away he got, the harder it was to see him. Eventually, she had to just sort of guess where Clark was.

When she was pretty sure he'd had enough time to

reach the shadows on the far side, she took a deep breath and crept forward and up the short steps leading to the elevated loading dock. She tried to remember to breathe normally. With no one in sight, and knowing she was virtually invisible to the cameras, Quinn drew herself up with newfound confidence and walked over to the doors. Each had a large square window filling the upper half. The doors were locked, but she leaned forward and peered inside the dark hallway on the other side.

When she was sure she didn't see anything in there, she looked over her shoulder and motioned for Clark to come up and join her. As soon as she turned, she saw a trio of hulking dark shapes emerge from the shadows directly behind where she thought Clark was standing.

"Clark, behind you!"

A flash of silver caught the floodlights just before Clark became visible. He'd drawn his sword.

Growling snarls filled the alley as the three dark forms charged the hunter. Quinn didn't have time to admire Clark's style with a sword. Snarling growls from behind sent her diving to the side to avoid the charge of two were-wolves as they burst through the doors.

Rolling to her feet, now fully visible, Quinn drew her silver Bowie and brandished it at the massive hairy beasts in front of her.

The pair split up, moving in opposite directions on the broad, flat loading dock to try to get behind her.

Quinn couldn't keep them both in her sight, which was a bad thing. She picked the one to her right and charged, drawing on her stamina to boost her speed.

The suddenness of the attack caught both creatures by

surprise. Quinn scored a deep slashing attack on the wolf-creature before dancing away from the beast's clawed counterattack.

She remembered its companion in time to duck under a leap that would otherwise have had its snapping jaws closing on the back of her neck.

As she ducked, she stabbed upward, and a wailing howl of pain rewarded her initiative.

Straightening from her crouch, Quinn squared off against the pair of now-wounded shifters. In a moment of foolish bravado, she pointed at the one on the right with her knife. She beckoned for it to come and get her with her free hand.

Instead of just the one, the pair charged at the same time.

Quinn realized she'd conceded the initiative. In a desperate move, she tried to leap straight up high enough so the two passed below her. It worked for one of her attackers. However, the werewolf on the left jumped to meet her. The two of them crashed into the brick wall of the loading dock.

The pop in her chest upon impact told her she'd probably just broken a rib. She grunted in pain when she landed but managed to stay on her feet.

The werewolf wasn't so lucky. The impact with the wall stunned it, and that gave her an opening to stab its neck. She drove in her twelve-inch blade to the hilt. Its howl of pain turned into a gurgling, choking sound as a flood of blood poured from its mouth. The werewolf began to shift to human form as it died.

Quinn yanked her blade free and turned to check on

the other wolf. It had recovered and was advancing on her again.

Now that the odds were even, the other beast was more cautious. Quinn took advantage of the stalemate to steal a glance at Clark. Judging from the two naked human forms lying still in the alley, he'd taken out two of the beasts.

Quinn was starting to think she and Clark had this in hand when distant howls sounded from inside the building.

"Clark, more are coming. We need to get out of here."

"Get back to the car if you can. I'm a little busy here."

Quinn focused on her stamina. The bar was about half-full and had turned a faded yellow-green color. She had room to try something.

Drawing on the boost even more, Quinn gathered herself and crouched just as the werewolf facing her charged.

Launching herself into the air from the loading dock's edge, she arched her back and sailed out into the alley to land on one knee nearly fifteen feet away, facing the rear entrance. Damn, she thought, that must've looked freakin' epic.

Clark's voice beside her startled her out of her reverie. "Don't congratulate yourself yet. We need to get out of here."

Quinn would ordinarily have been upset by Clark's typical buzzkill, but she was still impressed with herself. This would have been successful if it weren't for the impending reinforcements. The sole remaining werewolf had darted back inside rather than face both hunters.

"Which way?" she asked.

"Follow me."

Quinn nodded and started after Clark. She could tell he was injured, possibly severely.

She picked up her pace and caught up to him with ease. "Hey, are you all right?"

"Yeah, just a few scratches."

Quinn glanced at the drip of blood on the pavement. "It doesn't look like just a few scratches."

"We don't have time to do anything about it anyway. Let's get back to the car so we can get out of here."

A loud howl behind them, followed by a series of barking yips, announced that the rest of the pack had arrived at the loading dock. A chorus of howls followed immediately, and Quinn didn't have to look back to realize they must have found Clark's blood trail.

Quinn glanced ahead, trying to judge the distance to the car against the potential pace of the pack of uninjured werewolves behind them.

It was going to be close.

She was right.

They raced up the stairs and made it back to Clark's car just in time.

He pressed the keys into her hand, nearly collapsing beside the vehicle. She lifted him under one arm and helped him in as he climbed into the back seat and collapsed across it.

Quinn jumped into the front and gunned the engine to life, then backed out of the space and peeled out, heading for the ramp to the lower level. A werewolf jumped onto the hood as she drove, snapping and snarling, its drooling jaws on the other side of the glass from her face.

She didn't miss a beat.

She slammed on the brakes, then reversed, and the beast flew off the car's hood to land in a heap twenty feet down the ramp.

A grunt from the back reminded her about Clark. She glanced in the rearview mirror. He was climbing back onto the seat because the sudden stop had sent him to the floor.

"Seatbelts on for safety, please. This isn't over yet."

Quinn didn't wait for an answer. She stomped on the gas and raced forward, wincing a little as the car rumbled over the werewolf lying prone in the lane.

Then she drove straight for the street outside the garage, not bothering to stop and pay at the automated exit. The speeding sedan crashed through the wooden crossbar blocking the ramp, sending it spinning through the air as she snapped it off on the way through.

She turned left and picked the first exit that led onto the interstate winding through the center of the city.

Quinn checked the rearview mirror again to see how Clark was doing. He now sat upright on the passenger side. His seatbelt was on.

"How are you doing back there?"

"Better now that we're out of there in one piece. Good driving, even if I did break my nose against the back of your seat when you stopped."

"Sorry about that."

"Don't be. We got away. That's what's important. Plus, we learned what we needed to. That is definitely the right place. Those shifters were hired muscle to keep an eye out for us. Now we need a plan for how to get past them and inside."

Quinn smiled as she drove north back to the farmhouse. She'd gotten two compliments from Clark in one night. Things were looking up.

CHAPTER TEN

"Hold still, silly," Miranda snapped. "Don't be such a baby."

Quinn hid a smile behind her hand as the witch wrapped the bandage around Clark's arm where the shifter had bitten him.

"It'll heal well enough on its own. I told you I..."

"Hush," Miranda replied. "It was bleeding so bad that you might not have lived long enough for your super-human hunter healing to work. I'm almost finished anyway."

"I've survived worse," Clark muttered under his breath.

Miranda shook her head as she finished with the roll of gauze and used a strip of white tape to hold the end in place. Leaning back to check on her handiwork, Miranda smiled.

"There, now you can heal up, and there will barely be a scar."

Clark muttered something else under his breath. It was so low that Quinn didn't think Miranda or Taylor heard it.

The words were clear enough to her enhanced hunter hearing, though.

"But I like scars."

Quinn had to mimic a choking cough to cover the burst of laughter that escaped her. She didn't do a very good job, apparently.

Clark scowled at her. "Don't you have to clean our blades after that fight?"

"Uh, yeah, good idea. I'll get right on that."

Quinn went over to the sink, where she used a damp cloth to wipe the dried blood off the two weapons on the counter. Then she used a rag with a few drops of oil to coat the blades with a thin film of protectant to prevent rusting and pitting from the moisture and exposure to blood.

Nearby, Taylor leaned against the wall, watching Miranda fuss over the hunter. "You got bit by a shifter, right? Does that mean you're going to turn into one? That would be cool."

"No, it would not be cool, and I won't change anyway. Hunters are naturally immune. It's part of our inherent magic."

Taylor deflated once her hypothesis was shot down. She wasn't wholly deterred, though. "That is a thing, though? People can get bitten and turned into werewolves."

Clark sighed. "Yes, it's a thing, but the vast majority of shifters live happy, peaceful lives alongside their human neighbors without anyone being the wiser. For all you know, you could've grown up next to one yourself."

That got Taylor thinking. Quinn could almost see the wheels turning in her mind as she mentally went down the list of people she'd lived next to growing up. She wasn't going to let this go, despite the clear clues that Clark was done with the topic.

Knowing her friend better than the others, Quinn jumped in to change the subject. "So, Clark, what's next? We can't go in the front, and the back is guarded, too. How do we get in there and find out what's really going on?"

"I'm not sure. Give me some time. I'll come up with something."

"What we need is to know is the specific moment they're operating their VR system," Taylor said. "That would alert us to a pending attack, and we'd have a chance to stop them. I've been able to track usage over time, but not specific spikes when they're online. I'd have to be very close to the building or even inside and on their network to detect that."

"How are we supposed to do that?" Clark asked. "We can't camp out near the building and hope we get lucky. They've got too much security for that. Plus, they must have gotten a good look at Quinn and me during our scuffle with the shifters."

Taylor twirled a curl and said, "It would be easy if we could install a tracking worm in their system. Too bad you two can't go back and get inside."

Clark smiled for the first time since they'd returned to the farmhouse. "What would it take to install that tracking thing? Would it take long?"

"It's a worm, and no, it wouldn't take long, not if we could get access to the central server drives. I wouldn't need direct access. If we could slip a corrupted signal booster near one of their network hubs, I could hack in. Once through their firewall, I could install the worm in about ten seconds. I could show you how to do it. It's easy."

"I'm not going to do anything," Clark replied. "You are."

"What?" Quinn asked. "We nearly got killed trying to sneak in there. There's no way Taylor would survive."

"Wow, thanks for the vote of confidence, Quinn."

"I do not doubt you and your skills, but they're skills with the computer stuff, not fighting angry shifters and demon-possessed people. You've got no magical protection at all."

Miranda jumped in. "Wait a minute and think about this. Maybe Clark's on to something here. Perhaps her lack of magic and any supernatural connection is a bonus. She wouldn't trigger any safeguards they might have in place, and there are dozens of businesses in that building. They can't keep their employees and customers from coming in during normal business hours."

"So, we just send Taylor in there in broad daylight?"

"It might be the safest time to go," Miranda explained. "She'd be just another mundane among hundreds coming and going."

Clark looked at Taylor. "Would you be able to hold up while you go inside? It wouldn't be completely without risk, but we *must* find out what they're up to and when they're sending out slayers into the city."

Taylor nodded. "I can do it. Like I said, all I need is a few seconds alone near one of their communications nodes."

"But how do we get her inside without arousing suspicion?" Quinn asked. "She can get into the building, posing as a customer or employee of another business. That doesn't get her into this brokerage place, though."

Clark thought for a few seconds and suggested, "Maybe she could pose as one of their employees."

Miranda shook her head. "No, the company isn't large enough that they wouldn't notice someone who didn't belong wandering around."

"Not if they were expecting someone new." Taylor turned and headed back into the dining room, sitting down behind the row of monitors on the table. She tapped a few things into the keyboard and smiled. "I'll just get them to hire me."

"Just for the day?" Quinn asked as she and the others followed Taylor into the dining room.

"Look," Taylor said, pointing at the right screen. "They've got a request on a job board for a filing temp. One or two days of work and they're paying a few dollars more than minimum wage. I can create a fake account on this temp site and apply for them to hire me for that short-term gig."

"You'd have to stay the whole two days and do the actual work," Clark said. "You up for that?"

"Sure, I could use the extra time to snoop around and see what else I can turn up."

"You don't want to draw attention to yourself," Quinn said. "Remember, it's possible that some of the VirSync people might recognize you."

"Not if I pull a "Clark Kent" and go for the nerd disguise. I've got those fake glasses I got for my Halloween costume last year. And if I dress for business instead of my usual awesome fashion sense, I'll bet no one will pay me any attention at all. I'll just be another office drone."

Quinn didn't like it. Taylor took a huge chance offering to do this, and she'd have no backup. If she got into trouble, she'd have to get herself out of it without any help from them.

"You sure you're up to it?" Quinn asked.

"I can do this. I promise."

Quinn glanced at Clark. He seemed almost eager, leaning forward with a gleam in his eye as if he had the target of a hunt in sight. He nodded and said, "Apply for the job and get that wormy thing ready."

Taylor tapped a few more keys to complete her profile and clicked a screen button on the temp site. "Done. They haven't gotten any other replies to the job post, so I suspect I'll get a call tomorrow to come in. Plenty of time to rig a small signal booster that'll let me hack their internal system."

Miranda yawned. It started a chain reaction with the others, and Quinn laughed. "I'm going to bed. I've had enough excitement for tonight."

Taylor got up. "I'll work on the tech and check on the job first thing in the morning. Fingers crossed."

Quinn kept the reservations she had to herself. Taylor seemed to have made up her mind, and Clark said they needed a way to track down the slayers sooner rather than later. He was right. She just hoped her friend didn't end up hurt or worse because of it.

Taylor rose first the next day, partially due to the excitement she felt surrounding this opportunity to do more than sit and work at her computer. She slipped on a sweatshirt over her t-shirt and headed down to check on things. It was unlikely she'd get an answer so quickly on her fake job profile, but there was always a chance some manager was an early riser and checked the job board.

She started the coffee maker and then walked into the dining room and tapped on her space bar to wake up her system. After leaning over the table and typing in her admin password, she waited while the computer woke up.

A notification popped up in the corner of the center screen. Taylor smiled. She bounced on the balls of her feet as she clicked on it and waited for the job site to load.

The answer showed up at the top of the messages for "Jeanne Swift," the fake name on the account she used to apply for the job.

Ms. Swift, thank you for your interest in the filing job. Please respond with your earliest availability to begin. Pending your success at the initial interview, we'd like you to start immediately.

Taylor tapped on the accept button. A window popped up for her to answer.

I'm available immediately. Please email with the address and information for the interview and job.

She straightened up and returned to the kitchen to get some coffee. She had a lot to do to get ready for the interview. First up was to pick the perfect outfit. She had to look the part of a young professional eager for a job. It wouldn't do to appear as the rogue shadow-hacker she pictured when she thought of herself.

Taylor poured some coffee and headed back up to her room. She hadn't been able to get much in the way of new clothes since they'd gone on the run, but she'd managed to pick up a few things.

Her phone buzzed with a message before she got all the way upstairs. A quick glance brought a smile to her face. She was in. They wanted her there the next morning at 9 AM.

She had one day to build the signal booster and get herself presentable. She was now Jeanne Swift, office professional.

CHAPTER ELEVEN

It was sunny the next day when Taylor got out of the car a few blocks from the office building. They'd all decided it would be best if it looked like she was walking from the light rail stop. It would match the fake apartment address in Timonium she'd given them.

"We'll be close by if you get into trouble," Quinn said, leaning out the passenger window as Taylor straightened her skirt to keep it from riding up after she got out.

"I'll be fine. I'll text when I'm on the way back out this afternoon. Pick me up back here by the rail stop?"

Quinn nodded. "We'll be here. Good luck."

Taylor smiled. "Relax. I've got this." She turned and started down the sidewalk to the corner where she waited with a horde of other cubicle warriors heading to their ordinary jobs in drab offices somewhere nearby. Of course, they weren't about to help save the world like she was.

The bounce in her step buoyed her spirits, and she had a huge grin on her face when she arrived at the office building. She walked into the lobby and checked the board on the wall listing all the businesses with their floors and suite numbers.

Handon Services, LLC, was on the eleventh and twelfth floors. It looked like they had both levels to themselves. She checked her phone, reviewing the email she'd received from someone named Zelda. It directed her to head to room 1104 on the eleventh floor for her interview.

Taking a deep breath, Taylor headed for the bank of elevators in time to catch the next one as the doors opened. She stepped inside with the three other people waiting there and ended up near the back of the car. She asked the man standing by the panel of buttons if he could push eleven for her.

He turned and smiled at her, "You have an appointment with Handon Services?"

Taylor couldn't find her voice for a second. The man by the panel was Myles Hickman, head of VirSync and evil cult leader. He looked different somehow, grayer hair and a few more lines on his face and brow, but it was definitely him.

She straightened her glasses and said. "Uh, yeah. I'm hoping to land a temp job I applied for. They were looking for a file person for a few days. It's not exactly what I'm looking for, but I'm hoping it might turn into more than that. First things first, though, you know, right?"

Taylor resisted rolling her eyes at the way she just yammered on when she was nervous. She had to calm herself. She'd only met Mr. Hickman once back at VirSync, and she doubted he would remember her from among the dozens of VR candidates who'd been present that day.

Except he did recognize her, sort of.

"Do I know you? You look familiar."

"I don't think so. I'm new in town. I came in from Philly a week ago, which is why I haven't gotten a full-time gig yet. I don't suppose you know anyone up there I could talk to about something more long-term?"

Taylor pulled her hand away from her face. She kept fiddling with her glasses, which were an integral part of her disguise. Quinn would never let her live it down if this didn't work because she took her glasses off and someone recognized her.

Of course, if it didn't work, Taylor might not be around to worry about it.

"As a matter of fact, I'm very close to the CEO, Mr. Handon. I'm heading up to his office on twelve. If you give me your name, I'll make sure to mention the astute young woman I met on the way up this morning."

Her hand shot out to shake hands as she said, "Jeanne. Jeanne Swift, sir."

"Myles Hickman." He took her hand in his and shook it in a firm but not too tight grip.

The elevator chimed, signaling it had arrived on the eleventh floor.

"Thank you, Mr. Hickman. I hope we get the chance to meet again. I think this is my floor. I have to hurry to get to my interview on time."

"Best wishes to you, and good luck with the interview."

Taylor nodded her thanks again. She hurried away from the elevators down the hallway as she looked for her room. Thankfully, she had turned the right way and spotted 1104 on a sign beside one of the many doors lining the corridor. Below the number, the sign read, "Human Resources."

Taylor turned the knob and stepped inside.

She'd entered a small waiting area with four chairs and an open door on the far side.

A dark-skinned woman of about thirty-five sat behind a desk in the next room and smiled when she saw Taylor. "You must be Jeanne, am I right?"

"Yeah, that's me."

The woman got up and rushed to the outer room. "Thank you for coming in so quickly. This interview shouldn't take too long. As soon as I do a final check of your information, I'm sure we can get you to work and earning a little something your first day. Sound good?"

Taylor nodded and returned the woman's smile. "So, the interview is…"

"Oh, it's really just a formality to make sure we don't hire a serial killer or someone out to steal corporate secrets. You don't look like you'll be a problem in any case."

"I'm Zelda Kane. I head up the human resources department here at Handon. Oh, who am I kidding? I AM the human resources department, so let's just sit and chat for a bit, and then I'll check your application one last time. I'm sure you'll be able to start before lunch."

"It's nice to meet you, Ms. Kane. I'm happy to hear you think I'll work out. I could really use the job."

"We all need a good job; that's the best part of what I do. And call me Zelda. I insist."

"Okay, Zelda. Should we sit out here or in your office?"

The woman pointed behind her at the doorway and laughed. "That tiny space hardly deserves to be called an office. Besides, I prefer to walk and talk. That way, I get my steps in." She tapped the exercise watch on her wrist with one hand. "Follow me and interrupt me if you have any questions."

Taylor nodded and followed the woman out the door and back down the hallway to the elevator. Zelda pulled open a door just across from the bank of elevators and held it for Taylor.

"Come in here and see the nerve center for things here at Handon Services."

The next room was huge; it must've taken up most of one side of the whole floor. Inside were rows of low cubicles with dozens of people all talking at once on identical headsets. A set of large flatscreen monitors filled the far wall with numbers and letters scrolling across them in patterns denoting the various international and domestic stock markets.

"This is the call center where our associates reach out to potential investors and secure their trust, and eventually their money."

She and Zelda walked among the cubicles, and Taylor noticed right away something was off. None of the people talking on the headsets paid any attention to either of them. Surely someone would be curious about the newcomer. Some of the guys and even a few of the girls should be checking her out given the way Taylor knew she looked, but nothing—not so much as a peek or sideways glance, as far as she could tell.

If she were doing a monotonous job like making phone calls to random strangers, she'd take every opportunity she could for distraction.

Weird.

"They all seem so, uh, focused."

"Who, them? Yes, well, that's normal here. It's because their jobs might depend on the next sale they make. They're the stock and bond traders, and that's a tough job to break into. Mr. Handon personally interviews each of them before sending them down here to work. He puts tremendous pressure on them. He believes they must be molded in a crucible of fire so they can match up to the big brokerages on Wall Street."

"Their jobs are on the line?"

Zelda shook her head, flicking a hand dismissively as she walked along the row of cubicles. "Only the one with the lowest sales each month is fired. It's for the best, really. If they can't sell more stocks or bonds than the next trader, they're not cut out for this type of work. We lose a trader each week. They're sent up to Mr. Handon to explain their failure, and we don't see them down here again. He just sends them home. I've offered to send them an exit survey, but Mr. Handon says not to bother."

Taylor glanced over her shoulder at the traders as Zelda led her down a long hallway. She didn't care what kind of job it was; somebody should have looked.

It reminded her of the way Quinn described the effect of the spells VirSync had used against them. She couldn't remember it, of course, because the magic had worked on her. Maybe some sort of magic was at work here, too. She wished there was a way for her to be sure. If only she could cast a simple detection spell. Of course, that was why it was her sneaking in here and not someone else. She didn't have any magic of her own to be detected.

Taylor turned to the front as Zelda led them past a row of eight doors with hasps and padlocks on them. Taylor pointed at them and said, "Is that where they keep all the money or something?"

"Oh, no. All the money here is handled electronically. No, those rooms are for a friend of Mr. Handon's who needed some extra office space for a special project. They come in here at night when everyone is gone and do some sort of high-tech computer work in there. Nothing for us to worry about. Your area is just up ahead here."

Taylor looked ahead and saw a room with rows of filing cabinets lining the walls. In the center was a long table with four chairs on each side.

"This'll be where you'll set up for the next few days. We are in the process of digitizing all our older files. Start at that filing cabinet over there. Pull out the files one at a time and run their contents through the scanner system in the corner. Make sure there are no staples or paperclips. Once the scanning is done for that file, type the file's identifier number from the label into the scanner interface and hit enter. Then put the file back and do the next one."

"That's it? The interview's over?"

"That's it. You seem like such a nice girl. Do this for a few days. If it you get the work done in a timely fashion, we'll see about hiring you for an extended period. There's a lot that needs doing here. I'll come back at lunchtime with some paperwork for you to fill out. In the meantime, the directions and checklist for your work are all here on the table. The scanner is pretty complex and has a lot of functions you'll never use. Just use the manual system and scan things by hand. I'll see you in a few hours."

Zelda turned and exited, leaving Taylor alone with the files and the humming of the massive industrial scanner in the corner.

She put her purse on the table and glanced at the scanner instructions. She was pretty sure she could figure out how to use it on her own, but there was no need to reinvent the wheel if they had a system in place already. It looked precisely like what Zelda described: mindless grunt work for a person with little or no work skills.

Taylor noticed the instructions didn't take into account the automated feeder and collator built into the scanning system. She could batch-load the files and then stand back while they scanned themselves. If she set up the records that way, it would allow her to start searching for where VirSync might have hidden the servers needed to run the VR rigs.

Taylor sighed. First, she had to get this tedious job started. She had to do a good enough job today that Zelda would ask her back, just in case she needed another day to locate the server. Taylor went to work, setting up the automated system.

CHAPTER TWELVE

Two hours later, Taylor turned away from the scanner and checked the empty file folders laid out on the table for the next batch. She'd come up with a system to keep it all straight. Every scrap of paper from those files was now in the automated feeding hopper and would run through the scanner. It would then collate them back into the proper stacks for her to return to the correct folder.

The system gave her about twenty-five minutes before she'd have to return and reset the job for the next batch. Doing that three more times would get her close to lunchtime and Zelda's return.

Leaving the file room once again, Taylor walked down the long hall and checked the eight padlocked doors, four each on opposite sides. They seemed to be locked up tightly, but maybe she could try to pick the locks. She looked up to check and make sure the traders were still glued to their screens. Taylor froze. Myles Hickman walked down the hallway toward her.

"Hello, Ms. Swift. I see you landed that position after

all. Good for you."

"Thank you, sir. I was just taking a quick break to stretch my legs and keep myself fresh. Filing is tedious work. I want to make sure I do it without any errors."

"Attention to detail is important, that is true."

He stopped at the last door and pulled out a set of keys, fitting one into the padlock and removing it before opening the door.

He turned and looked Taylor's way. "Is there anything else I can help you with?"

"No, sir. I was going to head back to my work. You have a good day, and thank you for mentioning me to your friend, Mr. Handon."

"I haven't had a chance to do that yet. You got this job all on your own."

Taylor nodded as Myles entered the locked room. She managed to steal a glance past him as he went inside. One of the VR rigs was set up on a padded bench beside a desk that had a stack of electronics and computer equipment. She smiled. She'd found the location of the VirSync systems. Now it was time to install the signal interrupter.

She hurried away so he didn't catch her peeking at the gear.

Returning to the file room, Taylor fished in her purse and pulled out the small gray box with a short, v-shaped antenna jutting from one end. A standard electric plug extended from the other. The last of the locked VR rooms shared a wall with the file room. She searched that wall and found a power outlet hidden in the corner beside the row of filing cabinets.

Stretching her arm into the gap between the wall and

the nearest filing cabinet, she managed to plug the box into the outlet. While it had a battery that would run for several days, having an uninterrupted power source would boost its capabilities and reach even more.

Taylor stood up and had just returned to the scanner when Zelda returned.

Taylor checked the clock on the wall, which said it was only 11 AM. "You're back early. Is everything going all right?" She hoped she hadn't been picked up on a hidden camera or something. They might have seen her place the device in the corner.

"You're fine. In fact, you've made an impression on Mr. Handon. He called down and asked to meet you. He said you're a friend of a friend." Zelda waggled a finger at her. "You've been holding out on me. I wouldn't have given you this grunt work to do if I'd known you were a personal friend of the boss man."

"I'm not. I met a man in the elevator on the way up, and he found out where I was applying. He must've put in a good word for me. That's all it is, really."

"Well, you must have made quite the impression. It's not all the time he calls me like that. I've only talked directly to him a few times before, so imagine my surprise when his name popped up on my phone."

"I didn't mean to cause any problems."

"It's not a problem at all. I wouldn't mind if you mentioned me in a kind way when you're up there on the twelfth floor, though. If it comes up naturally, of course."

"I can certainly do that. You've been awesome to me, and I'd be happy to say so." Taylor fidgeted. She'd done what she needed to do. Maybe this was her chance to get away without arousing suspicion. "I suppose I'll just head on up there, then."

"Exactly. We don't want to keep him waiting. I'll show you where to go." Zelda glanced at the stacks of files and papers. "You certainly accomplished a lot in the short time you were down here. No wonder he wants to chat with you. He was probably watching you the whole time."

"What do you mean?"

Zelda gestured up to the corner of the room above where she'd installed the box. "The security camera, silly. The information in these files is quite sensitive. Mr. Handon likes to keep an eye on everything down here."

A chill raced down Taylor's spine. "He was watching me? From a camera over there?" She checked the corner. It was unlikely the angle allowed a view of her when she'd plugged in the interrupter. Taylor breathed a sigh of relief.

"It's okay. You don't need to worry about it," Zelda said, misunderstanding Taylor's reaction. "I took a little while to get used to it, too. It is his company, after all. His name's on the door, so if he wants to keep an eye on things, that's his right, isn't it?"

"Uh, sure, I was surprised, that's all. Are you going to take me upstairs to meet him?"

"Goodness, no, at least not all the way." Zelda fanned herself with a hand. "Between you and me, it's a little dark up there decor-wise. No, I'll take you up to the floor and drop you off. Then I have to come back down. His assistant will meet you there. She's new to the job, just came in about a month ago. She's a bit brusque, but that's all. Her name is Cindy."

Taylor hesitated. What were the odds that it was THAT

Cindy?

"Come on. We don't want to keep the boss waiting. I've heard he doesn't like that."

Taylor nodded and walked out the door and started down the long hallway back to the trading room.

The people in the cubicles were still focused on their tasks as before. It seemed even more creepy now that she picked out the positions of the hidden cameras positioned everywhere around the room.

A few minutes later, Taylor stood in one of the elevators, waiting for the door to open on the twelfth floor. It was only one floor up. For some reason, though, the short ride filled her with dread.

Her mind returned to the wounds to Clark's arm and torso from the shifter attack he and Quinn had faced the night before. It reminded her that happenings here had deadly serious consequences.

Glancing at Zelda humming quietly to herself, Taylor's hand dipped into her purse automatically to find her only form of protection. Her fingers brushed against the tiny throwing knife Clark had given her. It seemed so minuscule now when weighed against what she might be facing in a few minutes. She realized Clark had been toying with her by giving her the knife. He knew it was a useless item and practically harmless when weighed against something like his razor-sharp short sword.

The chime pinged, and the door slid open. Taylor stared at the floor in front of her and saw a pair of black high heels and the cuffs of bright red slacks. She tilted her head up to see who waited for her and scanned past an exquisitely tailored pantsuit.

Then she met the eyes and was face to face with demon-Cindy, although her eyes looked normal now, not the solid black pools she'd had the last time Taylor had seen her. The sardonic smile on the woman's face was hard to read. Taylor almost stabbed a hand out to push another button to take the elevator to another floor—any other level.

"Thank you for bringing her up, Zelda. You may go now."

"Of course," Zelda said. The woman gave Taylor a nudge in the small of her back, so she stepped off the elevator. "Good luck, Jeanne."

The doors slid shut, leaving Taylor alone with the demon. She surprised herself by stepping forward and extending her hand. "I'm Jeanne Swift. I'm here to see Mr. Handon."

"Of course. Mr. Handon is expecting you. If you will follow me?"

Taylor nodded and fell in behind the woman who marched along across a large open lobby filled with plush leather furniture and built-in bookcases on the walls. The carpet initially seemed to be black, but after a few steps, she crossed an area where the sparse overhead lights were a little brighter. There, Taylor saw the floor was really a deep red in color. She could see what Zelda meant about it being dark up here.

As Taylor stepped forward, she hid a sigh of relief. Cindy didn't recognize her when the doors opened, and that was lucky, but then the last time they'd seen each other, Taylor had been naked and covered from head to toe with black painted runes.

Cindy turned her head and said over her shoulder, "Mr. Hickman was quite taken with you. When he mentioned meeting you earlier, Mr. Handon was interested in meeting you, too. He's always one looking for a fresh…uh, face."

Something in the way she said it unsettled Taylor. She kept her hand in her open purse and gripped the smooth metal of the silver knife. She felt a little ridiculous even considering it a weapon at this point, but it was all she had.

Cindy stopped at a set of tall double oak doors, carved in ornate patterns that seemed to trap the eye if you stared at them too long. Beside them sat a desk.

The woman cleared her throat and said, "Mr. Handon is inside. He'll call you when he's ready for you to enter. Farewell."

Farewell? Who even said that nowadays? It sounded so final. "You're not coming in with me? Will you be here when I come out?"

A disturbing smile crossed the demon woman's lips. "When you come out? No, I think not. I have things to attend to elsewhere." The smile remained in place as she turned away and left Taylor standing alone.

The chime sounded in the distance behind her. Cindy had entered the elevator. Taylor scanned the shadowy room, trying to see into all the corners. She could not penetrate the darkness, and her mind started making up all sorts of things that might be hidden there.

A deep voice sounded from the other side of the double doors. "Come."

Steeling herself, she reached out for the handle and opened the door, swinging it inward. The doorway led to a room filled with a long conference table. Padded leather chairs lined either side, matching the dark browns, reds, and black from the outer lobby. A matching oak desk graced the other side of the room. It struck Taylor that there were no windows visible, only floor-to-ceiling black drapes lining the wall where she thought windows would be. She couldn't be sure.

A deep, hypnotic voice coming from behind the desk said, "Welcome, young woman. Come closer, so I might see you better."

Taylor moved closer to the desk. As she neared it, she realized the black leather chair was occupied by a tall, thin man with ashen skin. His black sports coat and shirt blended into the background. The hairs on the back of Taylor's neck rose in some sort of primal warning.

Thoughts started roaming through her mind, including her breakfast and coffee this morning. She wished she'd had more to eat. It was strange she thought about that now, of all times. She tried to force her mind back to the task at hand.

"Don't resist, child. I want to know where a sweet morsel like you came from to appear upon my doorstep so unexpectedly. Myles was correct; you are definitely not who you seem to be."

Taylor realized the scrolling memories weren't floating by of her own doing. This man was causing it. Somehow, he could read her mind.

She fought to regain control, but it was like pushing back against a moving wall of water. No matter what you did, it just flowed around your fingers.

Taylor forced herself to focus, concentrating on mundane things like furniture and food in the memories floating by, trying to ignore images or memories connecting her to Quinn and the others. Perhaps she could shape the thoughts she let out. It was a desperate plan, but it was all she could do to resist what was happening.

Taylor concentrated on high school and her brief stint on the school paper when she thought she might want to become a reporter someday. She latched onto those memories and tried to push them forward to make them seem more current.

It worked.

"You're a reporter?" Handon stood behind the desk. "I must say it's been a while since one of your ilk penetrated my veil. How did you find out I was here? Tell me. I promise, when I feed on you later, I'll make it painless."

Oh, my God, Taylor thought. He was a vampire, a real one, and he planned on drinking her blood.

Taylor pushed forward the image of a book cover she'd read once about a girl who fell in love with a vampire.

"Bah! That drivel again. Humans have turned us into something more like the fae than the creatures of the night we truly are. Enough. I thought you might be here for another reason, but now I see you just stumbled upon me by lucky happenstance. The luck is all mine, of course. Come around the desk, my dear, so I can select the best place to sample you."

Taylor's legs moved as if made solid planks of wood. She fought against going closer to the creature but couldn't stop herself. She lurched around the desk until she stood only a few feet away from her ultimate doom. This was it. She was going to die here.

The vampire, John Handon, stepped forward until he

loomed over her. He leaned over, placing one hand on the oaken desktop as he tilted her head to the side with the other.

She found her eyes staring down. She saw his hand on the desktop beside her purse. Curiously, the hand inside it ached. Why did her hand hurt so much?

She lifted it out of the purse and it came free, still clutching the hilt of the short silver knife. The sheath had fallen away, leaving the blade free to glisten and reflect the single overhead light. The grip pulsed in her hand as if it had a mind of its own. It seemed like a signal meant only for her.

Cool breath passed over her neck as the vampire sniffed her skin. Any moment now, it would be over.

The silver blade glinted at her again, drawing her eyes back to it as she waited for the first sting of Handon's fangs. What did the knife want from her?

She squeezed her hand tighter, angry that she couldn't understand what she was supposed to do. The edge of the blade closest to her palm bit into her pinky, drawing the slightest drop of blood.

That was enough. The sight of the glistening drop of blood released something inside, giving her control once again.

Shrieking with fear, Taylor lifted the knife and drove it down into the hand resting atop the desk with all the force she could muster. The silver-infused blade hissed and smoked as it passed through the pale skin and sank into the thick oak of the desktop below.

Handon howled and batted her away, the blow strong

enough to send Taylor flying ten feet to slam into the wall beside the door to the lobby.

Dazed, she struggled to fight her way back to full awareness so she could understand what had just happened. It all seemed unreal.

Her knife still impaled the vampire's hand. The skin around it shriveled and blackened as tendrils of smoke drifted up around it. Handon struggled to pluck the blade out with his free hand, but every time he touched it, his fingers sizzled.

Taylor pushed to her feet and did the only thing she could think of: she ran for the open door and into the lobby beyond. She expected to encounter demon-Cindy, but the possessed woman was nowhere to be found. Only the empty reception desk awaited Taylor. Seeing no one, she headed back to the elevator.

She skidded to a stop and punched the down button. The doors opened right away, and Taylor bolted inside. She hit the button for the first floor and then stabbed the door-close button repeatedly, expecting the vampire to appear at any instant. His distant howling continued but drew no closer.

Finally, the doors shut, and the elevator started downward.

Tears streaming down her face, Taylor dialed Quinn on her phone.

"Taylor, are you all right?"

"No, I'm leaving. Just come and get me, okay? Hurry."

There was a pause, then Quinn came back on. "Leave the front of the building and turn right. Keep walking on the sidewalk close to the street. Don't stop. We'll find you."

"Quinn, there's a vampire in there."

"A what?"

"You heard me. A vampire."

There was another pause, during which Taylor thought she could hear another voice in the background. It was probably Clark.

"Just get to the street and keep walking. We'll be there as soon as we can. Don't stop for anything or anyone but us."

The line went dead and the doors opened on the first-floor lobby at the same time. Taylor dropped the phone in her purse and marched for the front doors. She expected the guards to stop her, but no one said anything.

Soon she was walking down the street, moving as fast as her feet could carry her and not break into a run. It wouldn't do to draw attention to herself. Who knew where that creature's minions might be?

Taylor made it three blocks before a car pulled up beside her and Quinn jumped out.

"Taylor, what are you doing? I've been calling for you to get in for nearly a block."

"Quinn, I..."

Quinn stared into her face for a few seconds and then nodded and pulled her to the car.

Taylor got in, hardly noticing Clark in the driver's seat. Quinn shut the back door and climbed in the front passenger seat, and the car pulled away from the curb. Clark headed for the interstate ramp. They drove back north to the farmhouse and safety...maybe.

CHAPTER THIRTEEN

Quinn paced across the grass outside the farmhouse. "Honestly, Clark, I've never seen her like this before. She's not scared of anything."

"If what she describes is true, she came face to face with an ancient vampire. That's enough to scare anyone."

Quinn looked past Clark's shoulder at the house. They'd come out here under the auspices of doing some additional training work, but it was really to discuss what had happened to Quinn's friend.

"You don't understand Taylor the way I do. I've never seen her afraid of anything. She doesn't jump when you leap out and yell, "boo." It's like she's impervious. She laughs through scary movies."

"Not anymore." Clark nodded toward the house. "You saw her in there. She kept going on about how she could still feel his chill breath on her neck as she stood helpless to do anything. I've seen it before, Quinn. When you come face to face with the thing that scares you the most, it changes you."

"But she's never been afraid of vampires. Ever."

"Not vampires, Quinn," Clark said. "She's afraid of being helpless to defend herself. I think it's PTSD from something that happened to her sometime in her past. Do you know much about her?"

"No, only what she's told me since we met when she sort of rescued me from the streets. How do we fix her?"

Clark shook his head. "Maybe we don't. It will likely take some level of professional help, which we don't have the time or the resources for, so…"

"So why are you telling me any of this? You're no help at all." Quinn had her hands set on her hips. Her anger started to boil over inside. She'd let her friend walk into a vampire's lair knowing all along it should have been her. She was the huntress, not Taylor.

"I'm telling you because we still need her. I need to push her to get back to work, activating that box thing she installed sooner rather than later. We know they're close to enacting their plan, and we have to try to get ahead of them somehow."

"Aren't you afraid the whole vampire attack thing was related somehow to why she was there? Maybe they realized what she was doing." Quinn said.

"Maybe, but I doubt it. Taylor did say the box was transmitting a signal. They wouldn't leave it in place like that. Plus, vampires are apex predators, and Taylor's an attractive and capable young woman. That's like catnip to an old vamp like him. She told you how she found out he watched all the employees who worked for him. He probably just saw her hard at work, liked what he saw, and decided he was hungry. It might have even been a sort of twisted compliment. He might have planned on turning her."

"You're just guessing. You can't be sure."

"No," Clark said. "But I can't just give up, either. The only way we win this is if it was a coincidence. I'm counting on that."

"Okay, what's the game plan?" Quinn asked. "I understand you need her to get to work. I'm not going to let you go in there and bully her, though."

"Hopefully, Miranda has been able to soothe some of what's bothering her most. She might be able to do something with her magic to help. Let's go see. We'll play it by ear. We need her to check on that box she left and finish up her VR rig. I want both of us to be able to go in there and do what hunters do best when evil is afoot. Those slayers have got to be trying to disrupt the Fae summit that's coming to town, probably by killing or kidnapping one of the attendees."

"Clark, let me take the lead when we get inside. I know her and how important all this is. I'll find a way to get her back to work."

Clark nodded. He and Quinn headed back into the farmhouse. Miranda and Taylor sat at the small table in the kitchen with steaming cups of tea steeping in front of them. They spoke in low tones as the other two entered. The conversation stopped, and Taylor turned to check who had come in behind her. She'd been crying; the damp streaks down her cheeks and red eyes gave it away.

She stood up to face Quinn and Clark. "Clark. I need a new knife, maybe two. Something bigger this time."

"Something bigger wouldn't have fit in your purse the way the last one did."

"Yeah, well, the one I had was barely able to protect me."

Quinn shrugged. "I don't know, Taylor, it seems like you made it work just fine. For all we know, he's still pinned to that desk downtown. You did really well for someone who faced down a vampire on her own. I'm not sure I could do it, and I'm the huntress here. You said he probably had a whole office full of telemarketing stockbrokers working under his mind powers."

Miranda cleared her throat. "It's called being a thrall. That's the correct term for when a vampire makes a human's will subject to their suggestion and control."

Quinn glared at Miranda. Now wasn't the time for a vocabulary lesson.

Taylor shook her head. "It doesn't matter what you call it. I don't know how he's tied up with the remnants of VirSync, but it's definitely there. I ran into Myles Hickman and saw evidence of what are probably eight full VR setups in there that they can use. There might be more elsewhere, but those were the ones I saw."

Clark nodded at Quinn, and she knew this was her opening. "About that," Quinn began. "You said you managed to get your gadget installed. How soon will it be ready to radio home or whatever you set it up to do?"

"It's ready now. I just have to log in to the computer here. Then we're all set. It shouldn't take me too long to penetrate their systems with the signal interrupter in place."

Clark stepped over to the doorway leading to the dining room and glanced at the table where all the gear was laid out. "So, you've got two full VR rigs ready to go?"

"Uh about that," Taylor said. "It turns out we only grabbed enough extra gear to cobble together one headset for the VR dive. I configured it for Quinn because she's been in before and knows what to expect. I don't know how you'd react to it."

"I'll be fine. I'm the one who's going in if there's only one, not Quinn."

Taylor paused and shook her head, "It's keyed to her brain scan. I found it in the software we jacked from one of the stolen drives. I think that's an essential part of the process. If we don't have one for you, it could be awful."

"What? A brain scan?" Clark asked. "Where am I supposed to get one of those?"

Quinn jumped in. "I think that's her point, Clark. Look, I'm good with it. I've been in there before, and I know what the slayers they send out will be able to do. The best part is I can now do even more. Plus, you've said I'll probably gain more skills once I'm back in there."

"Not alone."

"I was alone before. The best you could do was help me get Miranda away once I rescued her."

Miranda said, "It might work better anyway since you can remain in the real world while wherever Quinn goes, she'll eventually have to return here. If we can come up with a way for her to signal you once she's inside, you can jump in the car and head to her location to help. Then when we have to pull her out, you'll still be there to lock things down and help any victims out."

"How's she going to carry stuff with her?" Clark asked.

"I thought she could only appear with stuff from the arsenal supplied by the system?"

Miranda smiled. "That's the good news. Taylor and I think we discovered a way using the tech/magic interface to allow Quinn a limited number of items to transfer with her inside. It wouldn't be much, but at least she could take the real Bowie you gave her. Plus, that's actually enchanted and blessed, which will help inside when in battle. It's possible that maybe her phone will transfer through, too."

"How'd you manage that?" Quinn asked. "I figured that was a non-starter since VirSync wasn't able to do it."

"They may not have wanted to," Taylor suggested. "Since they could equip you with anything they wanted you to have inside the VR, they didn't need you or want you to take anything inside. Your amulet circumvented that somehow with its own magic."

Quinn's hand came up to brush against the amulet hanging in view around her neck.

"Taylor's right." Miranda continued. "That amulet is what gave us the idea to try it. It required some tweaking, but we think it will work."

"What if it doesn't?" Clark asked. "We don't want her in there unarmed."

Taylor shook her head. "She should just be able to dial up her regular equipment list and manually equip anything that doesn't come through. We've thought of all that. We're ready for her to go and get this done."

Clark stood silent for a long time, then he gestured to the dining room and the computer setup Taylor had created. "Then do what you need to do. I've got a feeling something is going to happen soon. We need to be ready."

Quinn smiled. The excitement of getting back into the VR system, this time on her own terms, had her buzzing with energy. She wanted to kick some more ass. The fight with the werewolves the other night had given her a fresh taste of what she could do, and she wanted more.

CHAPTER FOURTEEN

I t was a good thing Quinn was ready to go. As soon as Taylor got her hack in place, the surveillance worm pinged her computer. The VR systems downtown were firing up for a mission. It woke them all out of a dead sleep, thanks to the joint alarms Taylor had set up on all their phones.

Ten minutes later, they all stood around the dining table while Taylor tapped away at the keyboard, and Miranda went over the spells she would have to cast one last time.

Quinn stood off to one side in black jeans, black boots, a black t-shirt, and her leather jacket. Her Bowie hung down in the shoulder-holster under her right arm. The only other thing she had was the phone in her pocket and a wireless earpiece connected to it.

"How much longer," Clark asked.

"I'm coding on the fly here," Taylor snapped. "Let me concentrate, or I could send Quinn to the arctic circle by accident."

Clark started pacing around the room, circling the table. He pointed to it. "Quinn, you'd better get ready and lie down. As soon as Taylor says the word, we have to send you after them. They'll have a head start on you. Time is against us here."

Quinn climbed up onto the table and laid down with her head next to the three flatscreens. Her feet hung off the other end from the mid-calf down. Still, that was the best they could do unless she was going to lie down on the floor.

Taylor snapped her fingers. "Got it. Okay, they've sent four people in this time. From the profiles I can see in their system, they're each one of the demon-possessed candidates."

"Anyone we know?" Quinn asked.

"No, at least not well. I scanned the names. They're using people from among the older candidates who were there before us."

"Quinn," Clark said. "Even if you knew them, they're not going to listen to reason. Don't hesitate to kill them. They're damned already, so your soul is safe because you're now working in the light."

She turned her head and craned her neck around to see Taylor between the monitors. "Does it tell you who their target is, or am I going in blind?"

"All I can see is the two men and two women they sent inside. There's no reference to the target." Taylor glanced at Miranda. "You ready to do this? They've made the transit. We need to send you now. All I can tell is it's somewhere downtown, near the Inner Harbor and the stadiums."

"I'm ready."

Miranda looked down at Quinn, smiled, and laid a hand on her shoulder. "Don't worry. We'll bring you back at the first sign of trouble."

"No, that's what the phone connection is for. Leave me in there until I call for an extraction. If you take me out too soon, I might not be able to save whoever it is they're after."

Clark headed for the door. "I'll head downtown now. Call me when you have a fixed location for the target."

Quinn nodded and grabbed the VR visor and pulled it down over her eyes.

Taylor's voice came over the integrated headphones. "See ya in a little while. Don't hog all the fun."

Before Quinn could answer, Taylor activated the system while Miranda started chanting. Two seconds later, blackness crashed down around her and a wave of overwhelming nausea hit her. Her hands clutched her gut. Before she had a chance to vomit, though, there was a flash, and she was no longer in the farmhouse.

———

Quinn opened her eyes to find herself standing on a grassy hillside, staring at the lights of the city around her. Before she had a chance to get her bearings, she lurched forward. Quinn fell to her knees, spilling the contents of her stomach into the grass as the nausea that had started at the farmhouse completed its course.

She rested on her hands and knees while she spat to clear her mouth. "Damn, Taylor," Quinn muttered, "looks like you didn't get the gear dialed in as well as you thought."

Sitting back on her haunches, she glanced around and tried to figure out exactly where she was. Taylor and Miranda were supposed to have sent her somewhere near Baltimore's Inner Harbor tourist district. This wasn't it. She could see the water from the hill she was on so it could be nearby.

Standing and waiting for the residual dizziness to dissipate, Quinn took in the area around her. An old cannon, painted black, was mounted nearby pointed out over the water.

I'm on Federal Hill, Quinn thought as she realized where she'd landed. She didn't see the harbor area, so she must be on the northeastern side of the park. She turned and walked to the top, following the path to the far side until she could see the shops and restaurants that made up the two main structures of the Inner Harbor.

It was late, and most of the establishments were already closed. Still, the area was well-lit and recognizable below her. A chirp in her ear reminded her to check in. She patted herself down to make sure she had everything. A quick search confirmed her Bowie, the phone, and the wireless earpiece had all survived the transit.

Quinn reached up to tap the button on the earpiece as the phone chirped again. The connection opened.

"Quinn, can you hear me?" Taylor asked.

"I'm here. I landed on Federal Hill, just east of the harbor."

She realized they had her in a three-way call when she heard Clark's voice, too.

"Okay, I'm on the way. Track down the slayers and try to get to their target ahead of them."

"I know what I need to do. I'll check back in when I find out what's going on."

"We're monitoring you from here. I can see your brain wave pattern coming back over the connection."

"Good, be ready to bring me back in a hurry if I need it."

"Don't worry, we've got you."

Quinn reached up and tapped the earpiece to close the call and turned in a full circle, searching for any sign of the VirSync slayers. They should have arrived in the area just ahead of her. That meant they were probably still working to acquire their target. She had to be faster and get ahead of them.

"I need a map," Quinn said to herself, not expecting an answer.

To her surprise, a sort of transparent overlay showed up on top of everything she could see. It took her a few seconds, but she soon spotted her location as a small pulsing blue dot. With a bit of concentration, Quinn discovered she could zoom in and out and move across the map if she needed it.

Quinn decided to try out some of the things she could do in the old VirSync system and tried to activate her tracking ability in conjunction with the map. A bit more concentration and... Bingo! Four red dots appeared on the map. It looked like they were a few blocks away in the residential part of the Federal Hill neighborhood, heading south of her position. If she hurried, she could catch up with them.

She didn't want a fight, or at least not yet. She had to break through their search line and try to get ahead of them. Then she could search for herself and maybe track in on their target. Then she could get them to safety. First, she had to catch them, and that meant she needed speed.

Bringing up the stamina bar was almost second nature now. Quinn drew down about ten percent of the available energy and poured it into her strength and speed. She took off at a run, moving across the top of the hill at a blurring pace. She reached the first of the well-maintained brick row homes in this affluent neighborhood and darted down the first street.

A glimpse of a fire escape down an alley gave her an idea. She twisted at the waist without slowing, changing her direction in a heartbeat. The jolt to her legs caused a slight twinge of pain, but she ignored it.

Leaping from ten feet away, Quinn cleared the second-floor fire escape railing with ease. She didn't slow at all as she bounded around and up the next three levels until she stood atop the slightly sloped roof. She looked down the row of houses.

"This is insane," Quinn thought. If her plan worked, though, she'd run right past the slayers without them being any wiser.

Pushing off from the low parapet at the building's edge, Quinn ran along the peak of the attached rooftops. She got to the end of the row, and on pure instinct, leaped as far as she could.

Exhilaration filled her as she landed on the roof across the street. She resisted the urge to shout with glee and kept going. This was like ultimate parkour.

Just before the end of the next block, Quinn spotted the first of the slayers. The black-clad figure slipped from shadow to shadow in the street below. It was unlikely any of the residents would be able to see them. To Quinn, her vision enhanced by the huntress amulet, the VR system, or maybe a bit of both, the slayer appeared as clear as day. It looked like it could be one of the males.

Quinn looked ahead to the next cross street. She might be able to get across before the slayer got there. It wouldn't do for them to spot a person making superhuman leaps across a thirty-foot gap. They'd know something was up for sure.

She decided she could make it but drew down a little extra stamina just to be sure. She was down to about seventy-five percent remaining. Launching herself forward, Quinn pushed off at the last house and flew through the air.

The power of her jump took her farther than she expected and she overbalanced forward.

She managed to salvage it by converting her fall into a rolling somersault, but it ended with her coming up hard against the side of the next home in the row, which was one story taller than its neighbors.

With a groan, Quinn untangled herself from the jumble of leaves and trash piled up against the bricks.

A glance at her HUD map showed the line of red dots, just behind her. They were spaced out on separate intersections, probably so they could search better. The four slayers had just crossed the street she'd jumped over, so she had to keep moving. She needed to put some distance between herself and the others.

Once she was a block or more ahead of the slayers, she could risk returning to street level and start the search for their target. There had to be a clue she could pick up before they did.

Quinn stood and grunted at a flash of pain in her right knee. She did her best to push it away and started running again, this time at a limping lope. It hurt a lot and wasn't her top speed, but it still covered a lot of ground in a hurry.

She reached the end of the next row of homes and planted one hand on the roof's edge so she could vault down to a shed roof below and then to the ground.

Standing once again on street level, Quinn checked the map. The others were moving slowly, still in the block behind her.

They didn't have a trail yet.

Stepping out onto the sidewalk of the cross street, Quinn checked both ways looking for anything out of the ordinary, something that might say "Fae" to her. Of course, she had no idea what that might be. She'd never met a real fairy before.

If Clark were here, he'd be able to find it right away because he was so damned good at *everything*. She hated thinking about it, but maybe if she tried to focus on what he would do, she could zero in on it herself.

With a sigh, Quinn cleared her mind and looked up and down the street.

"What would Clark do?"

She took a deep, calming breath and froze. She'd caught a smell she'd never sensed before. It was like a cross between fresh bread and peppermint, which a weird combination for someone to be baking, even in this hipster-laden neighborhood.

Clark had been trying to teach her to trust her senses

during his drills in the basement, although he hadn't been able to get her to sense anything at the farmhouse, no matter how hard he'd tried. Here in the VR world, though, maybe she could.

Closing her eyes, Quinn inhaled through her nose.

There it was, off to her left. It felt...close.

When she opened her eyes, Quinn's gaze fell on a home that was larger than the rest, standing a little apart from the others. It even had a small yard out front.

She caught a glimpse of a face in one of the second-floor windows before it darted out of sight behind the curtains. Quinn still had time to recognize there was something magical about it. There had actually been a sort of glow around their features.

She knew right away she'd found the slayers' target.

Checking the street for any sign of the approaching slayers, Quinn jogged over to the home, jumped over the wrought-iron gate, and bounded up the brick steps.

She rang the doorbell and knocked as well for good measure. This was urgent. She had no way of knowing how long she had until trouble arrived. Clark was Lord knew how far away.

The heavy wooden door opened a few inches, and a man's face with a gray beard and mustache slid into view. "Can I help you, young lady? It's very late."

The peppermint bread smell wafted out at her.

"I don't have time to explain. You have to let me inside right now. There's great danger close by for you and everyone inside."

"Danger? Just call the police. I'm not going to let anyone

into my home, especially some young ruffian with a big knife hidden in her jacket."

Quinn didn't know how he'd spotted the knife beneath her coat in the dark, and she didn't care. They had maybe thirty seconds left before four trained killers showed up.

Pushing against the door with her augmented strength, Quinn charged in, brushing the man aside as she did. She turned and closed the door, turning the double set of deadbolts.

That might hold them off, if only for a bit.

She turned to find the old man brandishing a pirate cutlass. There was some rust on the blade, but it looked sharp enough.

"Hey, I'm here to protect you. Put that away."

The man shook his head. "You barge in here, armed for death, and you expect me to put down my weapon? Leave now, and I won't skewer you on this pig-sticker."

He advanced, and Quinn had to step to the side to avoid the lunge as she drew her Bowie. The old man proved to be pretty nimble. Despite the gray in his hair and beard, she saw cords of muscle in his shoulders and forearms. He had the strength and skill to make his attacks count if she wasn't careful.

She prepared to parry the next attack as the old man came at her, but a stern voice from the top of the staircase nearby stopped both of them.

"Hold!"

Quinn froze, as did the old man.

A tall, thin woman with a beautiful, stately face descended the stairs. She wore a pair of tailored black slacks with flared bottoms and an emerald green blouse, unbuttoned just enough to expose a hint of her ample chest.

Quinn, who'd had more than a few romantic trysts with both boys and girls, thought she was just about the most attractive woman she'd ever seen. She was also the person Quinn had spotted peeking from upstairs as she approached the home. There was a sort of glow around her head, and the peppermint-and-bread odor came from her. Her voice had the lilt of the Irish.

"Put your weapons down, Alistair. You too, young lady. I'll not have fighting in this home. It belongs to a friend, and I won't have it sullied by death and violence."

Quinn managed to find her tongue at last. "Well, then you'd better disappear fast. There are four demon-possessed slayers out there looking for this house. They'll be here any minute."

Concern crossed the woman's face and she brushed back a strand of golden hair, a bracelet of woven silver strands sliding back to reveal an ornate blue and red tattoo of a bird on the inside of her left wrist. "What? How? Where are they, and who are you?"

"They are no more than a block from here. They were sent by a cult involved with destroying all the hunter clans years ago. Now they are back and trying to execute some sort of takeover. I'm the huntress charged with finding you and getting you to safety, but we have to leave now. Where's the back door?"

"A huntress, hmmm. That is most interesting. We must talk more, you and I, but I think we should leave here first, as you suggest. Four of the demon-kinder would be a challenge for me, especially since I'm still weak from using my magic to travel here. Alistair, I believe her."

Quinn had never heard Clark use the strange term "demon-kinder." The fae woman had put the word demon together with the beginning of kindergarten. It sounded right, though. She decided it fit them.

The woman looked at the old man, who snapped to attention and gave a brief bow. "Let me show you to the rear entrance, young huntress. Then I shall gather my mistress's things for travel."

"There's literally no time for that," Quinn said as she followed the odd pair through the home. They reached a large kitchen, where they stopped at a door with a six-paned window set in it. A white lace curtain hung down over the glass.

Quinn charged past when she saw the door. She pulled it open and gasped as a large, shadowy form stepped into the opening.

The fae woman had already moved around Quinn before she could warn her. She bumped into the intruder's chest.

A hand darted out and caught the woman as she stumbled back, startled. The figure stepped into the light as he steadied the fae.

"Hello, Filippa," Clark said. "It's been a long time."

CHAPTER FIFTEEN

"Clark Hunter, it's certainly been a long time. I thought you were dead with the rest of your brethren."

"Wait, your last name is actually Hunter?" Quinn interrupted.

Filippa pointed to Quinn. "Is she with you? She's quite brash."

Clark smiled. "I remember you being that way when you were her age."

"You don't remember me when I was that age. That was millennia ago."

"You know what I mean," Clark replied. "If by brash you mean that she tried to get you to get the hell out of here, I'd suggest you listen to her. She's right. There's trouble coming, and it won't be long before it finds you ."

As if to punctuate the statement, a crash of glass from the front of the house alerted them to the arrival of at least one of their unwanted visitors.

"Time to go, Filippa," Clark said. "I'll explain as we get out of here. Bring Alistair along. My car's out back."

"What about the girl? You're going to leave her here to fight off a group of the demon-kinder alone?"

"She can take care of herself, and she has her own special way to get home."

Filippa turned to Quinn and offered the slightest of bows before saying, "Thank you for your warning and protection, Huntress. I shall not forget your service."

As soon as she finished speaking, the woman turned, gesturing for Alistair to follow, and headed out the back door into the night.

Clark pointed to the front of the house. "Keep them busy until I get far enough away that they cannot follow. Return to the farmhouse as soon as we're safe. Don't try to be some sort of hero. I'll see you there."

He left, and Quinn spun, drawing her Bowie. She slipped to the side of the doorway and waited for the intruders to come and search this part of the home.

A glance at the HUD map showed two of the red dots centered over her position. Two more had moved around the outside of the home. She hoped Clark and the others had gotten away. It was strange that she couldn't see him or those he'd left with on the display hovering in front of her.

A creaking floorboard drew her attention back to the danger all around her. She wondered how long she'd need to give Clark before she could bug out. Part of her, in the back of her mind, screamed in terror at facing four of the demon-kinder, as the Fae woman called them. They were strong and able fighters in person. Inside the VR system, who knew what abilities they'd gained.

Quinn planned to leap out and slash out with her knife

at the first one coming down the hallway. That didn't work.

The plan went south when the intruder dove forward into the kitchen, passing right under her blade and rolling back to her feet behind Quinn.

Quinn felt a tingle on the back of her neck, and her amulet flashed with a sudden chill. She raised her blade up and behind her head.

A powerful blow from the other's weapon clashed with her Bowie, which barely parried the attack. The force nearly dislocated her shoulder and would have beheaded her if she hadn't blocked it.

She ducked and spun, kicking backward as she did. A grunt of pain rewarded her move.

Finishing in a crouch, Quinn got her first good look at her opponent. She recognized the woman she faced as one of the candidates from an earlier group, but she didn't know her name. Judging by her glowing red irises, it didn't matter anymore. She was possessed.

"I know you." The rasping voice coming from the woman's mouth didn't match what Quinn had expected.

Despite the seriousness of the situation, Quinn started laughing.

The response wasn't what the other woman expected. She let her double-bladed ax drop a little as she asked, "Why do you laugh? Is it because you see the futility of facing me and my brethren here?"

"No, it's because you sound absolutely ridiculous. Hasn't anyone had the guts to tell you before this? Seriously, you need to make new friends."

Quinn realized she'd gained some initiative. While the

demon-kinder was distracted, she slashed at the arm wielding the ax while snapping a forward kick up as a follow-up.

It worked.

The woman was able to bat aside the attack with the Bowie, but the kick caught her by surprise as she leaned in to parry the first attack.

Her head bent backward when the huntress's booted heel connected with her forehead. The cracking of the bones in her neck transmitted up Quinn's leg as it fully extended.

The woman dropped as if someone cut the strings holding a marionette up.

Quinn stepped forward to look down, amazed by the power of her blow and the effect it had. To her horror, the eyes facing the ceiling shifted to the side to connect with hers. Although her body had been paralyzed by her broken neck, she wasn't dead.

The woman took a gasping breath and said, "You won't fool me so easily next time. I will heal, and we shall meet again."

Quinn shook her head and glanced at her Bowie. Clark had told her it was special—blessed, or something like that.

"You know, I don't think so, demon spawn. You need to go back to where you came from."

She reversed her grip on the broad-bladed knife and dropped to one knee, bringing her weight down behind the blow. She struck in the middle of the woman's chest.

The demon-kinder let out one last heaving sigh, then the eyes went still and unfocused.

Quinn didn't stay there looking at her dead opponent.

There was another in the house with her somewhere. She rose and started down the hallway, her blade held ready to attack or defend as needed.

The soft scuff of a foot on the carpet nearby warned her someone was coming down the steps. A voice spoke, also carrying the grating quality of one possessed by a demon. It seemed like it might be a man this time.

"There is no one upstairs. Did you find anything?"

Quinn charged the last few feet to stand beside the stairs. She thrust her blade through the spindles and stabbed deep into the man's thigh.

She pulled her blade back as the demon-kinder howled and lost his footing, tumbling the rest of the way down the stairs.

Racing forward, Quinn dove at the downed opponent, hacking down at the arm holding a broad-bladed longsword.

She almost severed the hand at the elbow. It was enough that the sword dropped free and slid across the hardwood floor to stop a few feet away.

Quinn pulled her blade up high to deliver the killing blow.

A fist snaked out with unnatural speed.

Quinn jerked to try to dodge the blow.

The punch connected with her upper chest just below her throat. It would have crushed her windpipe if it had landed squarely, and she'd be dying from slow suffocation right now. It was still powerful enough to cause her airway to spasm. For a few seconds, Quinn struggled to take in enough breath.

The man beneath her bucked his hips, lifting her into the air and sending her rolling to one side.

Quinn let the roll carry her all the way over and back up into a crouch. She still struggled to fill her lungs and tried to hide it from her opponent.

The tall, burly man rose and pointed his uninjured arm at her. "You are the hunter the high priest told us about. He was correct when he said you were a young one. I didn't expect you to be so formidable. I assume you dispatched my companion?"

"I did," Quinn rasped. Her vocal cords were bruised. "It wasn't much trouble. Not any more than it will be to finish you off."

"I don't think so. I sense more of my cabal coming now. In a minute or so, you'll be dead. Then you will truly be the final hunter."

Quinn growled. "Stop calling me a hunter. I'm a hun*tress*, something altogether better. It's time you understood that things are going to be different this time around."

The man laughed and waggled his extended finger at her.

She realized he was egging her on, trying to buy time for his reinforcements to arrive. A quick check of the HUD confirmed her suspicion.

There was one thing to try, and Quinn wasn't sure it would work. She needed more air than she was getting. The huntress figured she had about ten seconds to finish this guy off. Pulling energy from her stamina, Quinn siphoned some away from the rest and concentrated on her bruised chest.

In an instant, she could breathe again. The healing attempt had worked. That problem solved, Quinn used the remaining power draw to take two spinning steps forward. She delivered a crushing roundhouse to the demon-kinder's chest.

It sent him flying into the living room to crash into the coffee table.

She rushed in to stand over him as he struggled to rise from the splinters of the table. She lunged forward, stabbing at an angle so her blade slipped under the ribs and into the demon's heart.

He made one feeble attempt to swipe at her and then went still.

The kitchen door opened, and more demon-kinder voices called out in alarm. They must have found the one she'd killed.

Quinn figured it was time to get out of here. She tapped the button on the earpiece, which was miraculously still in place, thanks to the metal clip hooked around her earlobe.

The connection opened immediately, and Taylor's voice came through.

"Quinn. Finally. We've seen some strange readings coming in through the link. Are you okay?"

"Now would be a good time to get me out of here. I'm already pressing my luck."

"We're ready on this end. Get set. Here we go."

No sooner had Taylor's sentence ended than Quinn's awareness yanked backward as if pulled by an enormous bungee cord. The nausea and dizziness returned, followed by the wave of blackness.

She was on the way home.

CHAPTER SIXTEEN

Quinn woke up in the farmhouse dining room, flat on her back and retching once again. Her stomach rebelled against the magic and technology and tried to empty, although it already was. Miranda rushed over and rolled her on her side as she vomited again.

Luckily, she'd emptied her guts in Baltimore, so she only dry-heaved for a minute or so.

Taylor had moved from behind the monitors and held Quinn's hand, concern creasing her brow. "God, Quinn, that was scary. You all right?"

Quinn coughed a few more times and said, "I think you two need to work a bit more on dialing in the transfer process."

"Was it bad?" Miranda asked.

"Let's just say, I hope I don't have to go back in any time soon. I'm going to need a little time to recover. Plus, I have the migraine to end all migraines."

Taylor helped Quinn sit up and swing her legs over the

table's edge. "We'll try to refine the code and magic mix before the next time. You were successful, though?"

"Yes, Clark's on his way back with two people. One's a fae leader, I think. The other's her butler or something."

Miranda and Taylor steadied Quinn as she stood. Her head still throbbed, and her legs trembled beneath her, but she took a few unsteady steps on her own.

"I'm fine, I guess. I'm going to go up and wash off. Maybe a shower will help. I'll be back down soon. I expect Clark will be back by then, and we can talk about what we need to do next."

She headed for the stairs and climbed up to her room, where she grabbed some clean clothes and went into the bathroom. The hot water of the shower soothed her muscles. When she used her skills to boost her energy and strength, there was an effect afterward. It was like the day after a particularly hard workout in the gym when every muscle ached from exertion.

Quinn shut off the shower and climbed out when the hot water began to run out. As she toweled off, she heard Clark's voice downstairs. She couldn't make out what he said. Quinn hurried to get dressed. She decided to bring along the shoulder holster rig even though she was in the relative safety of the farmhouse. There was no telling what the slayer teams were capable of, and they were going to be searching for the ones who'd killed their brethren and spirited away their prey.

She shrugged into a t-shirt and blue jeans, slid into the straps of the rig holding her Bowie, and went downstairs.

Clark stood in the kitchen, leaning against the counter and talking to Filippa, Taylor, and Miranda. He smiled when she walked in. "Glad to see you made it back in one piece. How'd you fare against the slayers?"

"I managed to kill two of them. The other two I left behind before they found me. I think we passed along our message."

"Did they see you?"

"No, I located them using my HUD and bugged out before they got all the way into the house."

"You had a HUD inside the system?" Taylor asked. "I didn't code that in for you. It must've been in the code I copied from the VirSync drives. I'll have to go look."

Clark nodded. "It could be her strange affinity, too." He turned to Quinn. "Anything else unusual or special pop up while you were inside?"

"I got that tracking-by-other-senses thing working. You've been trying to awaken that in me for a while. I got near the house, and I sensed Filippa. That allowed me to narrow in on her location."

"You sniffed me out?" the fae asked with amusement. "I hope it was a pleasant odor."

Quinn smiled. She inhaled and caught the faint hint of peppermint and baked bread in the air. "Definitely pleasant. Don't worry."

It appeared that she'd once again retained an ability gained while in VR. On a whim, Quinn tried to bring up the HUD by concentrating on their location and visualizing the surroundings. A faint transparent image appeared over her visual field, and she tried to focus on it. It solidified some, but it wasn't as easy to see as inside the VR world.

Quinn could see the farmhouse and its immediate

surroundings out to about a hundred yards, with her location shown as a pulsing blue dot in the farmhouse kitchen. She tried to zoom out to a broader view of the area around them but couldn't do it. There were apparently limitations to this new ability. Still, it could come in handy on this side of the interface, too.

"What's up, Quinn?" Taylor asked. "You had a faraway look in your eyes for a bit there."

"I was just thinking about something." She decided to keep the new abilities to herself, especially with guests around. Maybe she would tell the other clan members later when they were alone again.

"I find this talk of technology and magic working hand in hand fascinating," Filippa said. "In my experience, the two have always been mutually exclusive. One has always canceled out properties of the other in close proximity. You seem to have conquered that."

Taylor smiled but shook her head. "We can't take credit, though we're taking advantage of it. We stole the tech and spell combination from the bad guys."

Clark nodded. "That is how they're able to get so close once they localize you to an area. They use the tech to project their slayers directly to you for the attack. There will be virtually no warning before they initiate an assault."

"I saw that when your huntress here showed up on my doorstep only a few hours after I'd arrived. You say the others can do this, too?"

Quinn nodded. "I killed two of them in the house before I returned. They tracked you to that neighborhood and were searching for you when I arrived. We think they can send up to eight at a time. We only have the capability to send me right now."

"Hopefully," Clark added, "we'll be able to expand that shortly. We'll have to be able to match them."

Quinn could tell from the scowl crossing Taylor's face that she didn't think they'd be adding more VR rigs anytime soon. She'd said the tech was complicated, and she had only been able to create what they had with pieces they'd stolen from the company leftovers.

Miranda asked, "Do I need to try to create someplace for the princess and her attendant to sleep?"

"You're a princess?" Quinn asked. "Like, a real fairy princess?" A smile crossed her face. Filippa didn't match the image she'd grown up with.

"I am, but you are not required to address me as such. You are not among my subjects. Even humans with supernatural abilities have long demonstrated reluctance to bend to our authority." Her glance in Clark's direction told Quinn she needed to learn more about his history with this woman.

Filippa continued, "I will not be able to stay here. The summit with the other fae must still take place, and I must assist with the details and planning."

"Filippa, we barely saved you back there. You can't return to that house." Clark's concern and maybe a little anger showed in his tone.

"I will not return there. That would be foolish, Clark. Give me some credit. Also, I'm not without protections of my own. I'll find a more secure location from which to manage preparations."

Clark started to say something and she held up a hand,

forestalling his answer. "I've made up my mind. You'll not dissuade me, so do not waste my time trying."

Quinn resisted the urge to smile. She could practically hear Clark's teeth grinding as his jaws clenched in an effort to hold his tongue.

He found his voice a second or so later after locking eyes with the fae princess. "Fine. I'll give you and Alistair a ride back into the city so you can get back to work, then."

"No need for that. Alistair has already reached out, and a vehicle is on the way here with a security team for my protection. We'll return to the city and get back to work."

Clark shook his head. "I wish you'd asked before sharing our location with anyone else. We've avoided detection this long. I had hoped to stay off the radar of the supernatural community a little longer."

"I assure you my contacts are reliable. You and your group are in no danger, at least not from us."

Clark clearly wanted to contradict her, but he didn't answer. Quinn knew it made no difference anyway. The damage, if any, was already done.

"Well, at least fill me in on the details of what you have planned for the summit. We can help provide security for you, as we've done in the past."

"No, Clark. I appreciate what you've done here with your huntress and the others. Sadly, however, you cannot resurrect the clans. The hunters are no more. The other fae would not trust that you could provide the protection we need. We must protect ourselves."

Her dismissal angered Quinn. "How can you say that? We just saved your ass. I risked my life for you, and you have the nerve to turn up your nose at us because we're not good enough for you somehow?"

Clark cautioned Quinn with a sharp rebuke. "Quinn, don't speak to her that way. You don't know all that has passed before."

"I don't care, Clark. What was the use of sending me out there to help if people like her are going to treat us like dirt?"

Clark started to say something, but Filippa stopped him. "Clark, why have you not taught her to curb her words around her betters?"

"Betters?" Quinn replied. "You think you're my better? You might be a whole lot older than I am. That's obvious. You're not my better, though. I've survived when no one thought I had a chance. I've been fighting the odds since I was born, so don't you stand there and act like you're somehow worth more than I am."

Filippa's eyebrows shot up and she smiled. "My, my, your huntress has fangs, Clark. I'd suggest you teach her some manners before we meet again.

A horn honked outside. Filippa nodded. "That will be our ride. I'll take my leave so you can attend to the issues in your house, Clark. Until next time."

The fae woman inclined her head in a slight bow and left.

Quinn waited until she heard the front door shut before saying anything. "How can you let her talk to you, to me, that way? WE saved her, not anyone else. She needs to get that stick out of her butt before I'll bother to stick my neck out for her again."

"Quinn, you spoke out of turn just then." Clark ran his

hand through his graying hair and shook his head. "The fae are prickly. You have to handle them carefully to get them to come around and do what you want them to do. I'd hoped to at least get an invitation to help with security. Now, we're going to have to try to protect them from the outside. We'll have no way of knowing what the hell they're up to."

"That's not my fault. She was rude."

When no one answered her, Quinn looked from Clark to Miranda and finally at Taylor, who only offered her a shrug in response.

"Fine, I'm the bad one. It's not the first time, and I'm not backing down. If she gets herself killed by slayers because of this, it's on her. I'm done protecting that particular fae princess."

Before anyone could answer, she headed back up to her room. She was tired and needed sleep to restore her strength. She also knew herself well enough to know she was about to say something that might be hurtful to her friends. She needed to cool down and get some rest. She'd address the implications of what she'd said with them in the morning.

CHAPTER SEVENTEEN

Quinn opened her eyes and stared up at Clark, who loomed over her bed. "Let me sleep, Clark. I'll talk to you in the morning."

"It is morning. I let you sleep in past eight, now get up. We've got work to do."

Quinn groaned. If Clark was telling the truth, she'd gotten nearly six hours of sleep. Given how wrecked her body felt as she stretched and sat on the edge of the bed, she decided it hadn't been nearly enough.

"I'll wait for you downstairs. Don't take too long getting yourself breakfast. I'll tell Taylor to start a fresh pot of coffee. You look like you need it."

Quinn opened her mouth to snap something witty back at him but stopped when nothing came to mind. Wow, last night had really thrown off her game. She got up and stumbled into the bathroom, where she splashed water on her face to try to wake up.

She returned to her room, changed into a pair of leggings, and tugged a t-shirt on over her sports bra. Clark had sounded like he planned on working her pretty hard this morning, and she wanted to at least be comfortable during the training.

By the time she arrived downstairs, the pot of coffee had finished filling. She grabbed a mug, the half-and-half, and the sugar bowl. After filling the cup a third of the way with cream, she filled the rest with coffee and added three heaping spoonfuls of sugar. She stirred the mixture a few times, pulled out the spoon, and popped it in her mouth.

As soon as she did, a series of images from the previous night flashed through her mind. For an instant, she saw both the demon-kinder she'd killed, their sightless eyes staring up at her. A shudder went down her spine, and she blinked until the images disappeared.

What the hell was that?

Quinn glanced around the kitchen and through the door to the dining room, where Taylor and Miranda were hard at work on something. Neither of them had noticed whatever it was that had happened to her. She put the strange feeling out of her mind and reached across the table for a banana. She didn't feel much like eating, but she knew she needed something in her stomach before the training began. She'd bring an apple down to snack on later.

"Hey, Quinn," Taylor said as she walked in to refresh her cup of coffee. "Clark said you looked rough this morning. He wasn't wrong."

"Wow, thanks."

"Hey, don't shoot the messenger. Did you sleep at all last night?"

"I think so. I don't remember waking up. I should feel a lot better than this."

"Miranda and I are working on cleaning up the interface software, and the spell commands she's using. She thinks she can ease the effects by adding healing runes to the headset. That should help fortify you the next time you go in."

"That's good, I guess." Going back in was currently the last thing she wanted to do. She couldn't tell Taylor that. She'd worked hard on this, and it would upset her if she knew how Quinn felt about it. "I need to rest up some, though, and recover my strength before I try that again."

Quinn saw she'd said too much, judging by Taylor's concerned expression. She added, "Hey, you know me. I bounce back fast. I'll probably be fine by dinnertime."

Taylor didn't look convinced, but she gave Quinn a half-smile and nodded. "I'll check on you later. Make sure Clark doesn't work you too hard down there. Tell him you don't feel well."

"I can't do that. If he thinks I'm slacking off, he'll just work me harder. He's all about pushing through the pain and going past my limits. I'm better off not saying anything."

"I could tell him we think the VR had an effect on you and that you need some time to recover."

"No, don't. I've got this. This is nothing worse than a hangover, and I've worked out and practiced through enough of those." Taylor knew Quinn had done precisely that after weekend parties back in high school.

"I'll talk to Miranda while you're downstairs. Maybe she has some magical suggestions to fortify you for the time being until you get caught up. We can try them out when you come up for lunch."

Quinn nodded as she got up. "I'll let you know. I'd better get downstairs and get started. I don't want him to come up and look for me." She finished her banana and threw the peel in the trash, then pulled the basement door open and went down to their makeshift training area.

Clark had rearranged the old canvas practice mats. Now, he had them doubled up in a smaller area than usual. Quinn hoped that didn't mean he planned on throwing her down doubly hard.

"Good, you're here. There's something I think we've been missing out on. Something Filippa said on our way home last night triggered a memory that I think might help."

"I'm not sure I'm interested in anything she suggested for me."

"It's not that at all. Come and sit down and I'll explain."

Clark sat down cross-legged on the far side of the mat and gestured to the area opposite him.

This was weird. They'd never done anything but work on combat techniques down here. The only conversations were one-sided with Clark on the talking side, giving critiques mostly.

Quinn sat with her legs crossed just like his. Maybe he was going to show her how to defend against an opponent when in this position.

"Good. I think I've missed out on sharing something with you, and I have to remedy that before we progress any further."

"Look, Clark, if you want me to apologize for blowing

up at your old girlfriend last night, I will, but only to you. I never intended to make it hard for us to do what we have to do to stop Myles and the others at VirSync."

"It's not that," Clark said. He chuckled. "And she was never my girlfriend. That would never have been allowed, at least not that way. We were friends for a while, a long time ago."

"Okay, now I have to ask. What the hell did she say to you that's got you all worked up like this?"

He chuckled. "Filippa made a comment that your— Well, let's just call it your direct nature reminded her of me. That was before training with her and another fae master in mediation techniques. I think that might be my fault, and it's something I need to remedy."

"Meditation isn't my thing, Clark. I'm more direct about how I deal with the world."

"Me, too, but there are things about being a hunter and some abilities that can't be unlocked unless you work at centering yourself and recharging."

"What, like a battery?"

"Sort of. Your power, and mine, all come from the earth and the world around us."

"I thought mine came from the amulet."

"No, that's just a vessel for power and certain spells that control that power. You, the hunter..."

"Hunt*ress*."

"Yeah, Hunt*ress*. Anyway, you can regain strength and even a limited regenerative ability through connecting with natural elements all around you. It's how you and I heal faster than others do—you draw on that energy without even realizing it. What I want to do is to help you try to boost that feed when you need it, like now."

Quinn didn't go in for all that crystals and pyramid energy stuff, but she'd seen enough strange things since this whole new world had opened for her that she decided to go along for now and see what happened.

"Start by closing your eyes and trying to see sources of energy nearby. There's a pretty strong ley line not far from this house. It was one of the reasons I selected this place. Try to sense it, and when you think you have it located, point in its direction."

Quinn did as she was told, unsure of what she was looking for. She reached out with her mind, trying to feel anything around her that might indicate a power source. She had no idea what she was supposed to see or look for. When nothing immediately popped up after a few seconds, Quinn tried something different. She concentrated and brought up the HUD map of the area around the farmhouse.

While it was restricted to the immediate area, the ley line was there. It sort of ghosted in and out across one corner of the map near where the farm's old windmill pump for the well was located. It appeared as a faintly glowing gold line passing through the property.

Curious, Quinn reached out with her mind and tried to pull power from it, since that was what they were here for. Clark had said she could draw on it for energy when needed. When nothing happened, Quinn's hand drifted up to touch her amulet, pressing it against her chest beneath the t-shirt.

This time, something happened. A thin offshoot of the

gold line bent away from the rest of the ley line and curved toward the farmhouse at the center of the map. Quinn smiled and pulled harder, focusing her mind on drawing in the energy.

Suddenly, power surged into her, energizing every muscle in her body. She felt immense power and agonizing pain as all her muscles fired and contracted at once, warring within her body to flex or extend her limbs. Since nothing could move with opposing muscle groups preventing it, she just trembled while the power coursed through her.

The whole thing only lasted a few seconds. It freaked Quinn out so much that as soon as she could, she let go of the power, allowing the curved line of energy snap back into place with the rest of the ley line.

"Quinn, what are you doing?" Clark asked. Concern clouded his face when she opened her eyes.

Before Quinn could answer, feet pounded across the kitchen floor overhead. Miranda and Taylor dashed down the steps and skidded to a halt at the bottom, staring at her.

"What's wrong?" Quinn asked. "Why are you all staring at me?"

Clark asked, "How do you feel right now?"

That was a strange question since she felt great. Clark had been right; that ley line power thing could recharge the batteries when needed.

"Honestly, I feel wonderful, better than I have in weeks. It worked just like you said it would."

Quinn twisted around to look at Taylor and Miranda. Taylor had her phone out like she was shooting a recording or something.

"Are you *videoing* me?"

Miranda reached out and tapped Taylor on the arm so she lowered her phone. Then she stepped forward. "You're sure you're all right?"

"What are you staring at me for? You're starting to freak me out."

Taylor reached up and tapped her phone a few times. "I sent you something. Check your phone."

Quinn reached for the phone on the mat next to her and saw it.

A golden nimbus glowed along the outline of her arm.

She snatched her phone and opened the message from Taylor. It was a screen capture of her seated on the mat. Her whole body was outlined with the same glow.

The hand holding her phone dropped to her lap. "What's that all over me? Why am I glowing?"

Clark said. "You didn't do what I told you to, did you? I asked you to point to the ley line. You did something else, right?"

"Yeah, so? I saw where you were going with the whole recharge thing, and I felt like crap, so I just kept going. I reached out to it and siphoned off some of the power."

"You reached out for it? That shouldn't be possible."

Miranda shook her head as she and Taylor came around to stand beside Clark. "I've never seen a person hold so much raw power before. It should have fried every cell in her body, but she looks fine."

"Tell us exactly what you did, Quinn," Clark ordered.

"I found the ley line like you asked, and then I sort of peeled a thin strip of it away and bent it toward me for a few seconds. I let go as soon as I felt the energy overload. Am I going to glow like this forever?"

Miranda said, "I don't know. It shouldn't be possible to manipulate raw power that way. The most I can do is siphon off a little from the periphery. Even then, I have to be a lot closer than this. To actually manipulate a line the way you did is impossible, or it should be."

"Apparently not," Taylor said. "She did it. Don't worry, Quinn. It's faded a lot since we came down a few seconds ago. Seriously, you were lit up like a light bulb. I got it on video."

"Uh, thanks, I guess." Quinn looked at Miranda and then Clark. "I didn't mean to break anything, honest."

Miranda was the first to laugh, and after glancing at her, Clark joined in. Taylor joined in as well. Quinn crossed her glowing arms and glared at them. She didn't think this was funny.

Her glare only fueled their laughter.

"What is so amusing? I'm, like, radioactive or something over here, and you all are treating me like I just slipped and fell or ran into a wall."

Clark gathered himself and sighed. "I'm sorry, Quinn. It was a combination of the look of horror on your face, combined with the relief we all felt that you were okay after what happened."

Completely missing the fact that Clark actually apologized to her, Quinn latched onto the last thing he said. "After WHAT happened?"

Miranda wiped at her eyes and answered. "Quinn, you touched a primal source of magic. Physically touched it.

That's the equivalent of grabbing onto a high voltage electric line with your bare hands.

"Apparently, it's not as bad as all that," Quinn said. "Other than this glow, I'm fine."

Clark shook his head. "It's every bit as bad as that, Quinn. I'm not sure how you survived it. No human should be able to. That kind of power would have burned any of us to ash. Instead, you held onto it and then just let it go."

Quinn held her hands out in front of her, staring at them. The glow had definitely faded in the last minute or so. It was barely visible now. "I didn't know. Did I break something?"

"No, things feel normal again outside," Miranda said after a brief pause where she closed her eyes. "You, on the other hand, are full of more magical energy than I've ever seen anyone hold before. I'm not sure how even though I'm staring right at you."

"It's fading, though," Quinn said. She lifted her arm. "I guess it's going away."

"Not really," Miranda said. "It's more like it's getting absorbed into your cells. I can still feel it when I focus on you, but now it's more internalized. Based on what I can sense, the glowing thing will go away completely in an hour or so, I'd guess."

"What's this mean?" Quinn asked. "If you both say no human being can do this, what does that make me?"

Clark shot a look at Miranda. Quinn didn't miss the minute shake of his head. The witch didn't respond other than purse her lips for a moment. She looked as if she was about to say something.

"Come on, guys. What kind of freak am I?"

"You're no kind of freak," Clark said finally. "You're a hunter apprentice who needs to follow instructions next time so this doesn't happen again. Got it?"

Quinn didn't even bother to correct his use of hunter instead of huntress. Something about what happened had Clark and Miranda concerned, and it appeared they knew more about it than they let on. It was also clear she wasn't going to get answers from them right now.

"Fine, I'll listen better next time. Now can I go upstairs, because I'm suddenly starving? I think I could eat everything in the fridge right now."

"That's a good idea. While you're eating, Miranda and I will go out and do some shopping. Eat as much as you want. We'll get more."

Quinn didn't care that they were being so obvious about getting away so they could talk about her. All she wanted right now was food. She'd get answers from them later.

CHAPTER EIGHTEEN

The glow along her skin faded soon after she went upstairs and ate something. Quinn double-checked to be sure by going into the closet near the front door and closing the door. In the total darkness there, she checked every inch of exposed skin in the dark to make sure she didn't glow anymore.

Relieved that it looked clear, she came out and returned to the rest of her lunch. As she made a third sandwich from the remainder of the deli meat they had in the fridge, Taylor watched with an amused grin on her face.

"What?"

"I've never seen anyone put away that much food in one sitting before. We should sign you up for one of those contests. I'll bet we could win every one. We'd just have to find one of those power lines and jack you into it first."

Quinn took a big bite of her sandwich and said through a mouthful of food, "How would we explain my glowing skin to the other contestants?"

"Well, we'd have to come up with a timetable to make

sure you didn't freak anyone out. Still, you could become famous, like that hot-dog-eating guy."

"I don't want that kind of fame, thank you. I don't plan on doing that ever again. It wasn't a pleasant experience."

"You look like you feel better than when you went down there. Maybe you could recharge like that after every trip into the VR now?"

"No, thank you. Who knows what that did to me? It could've scrambled my genes or something. I have a better idea. Why don't you and Miranda go fix whatever's wrong with how you sent me through the last time, so I don't come back feeling and looking like a famine victim?"

Taylor flinched at Quinn's tone, and the huntress regretted saying it as soon as came out.

"Hey, Taylor, sorry about that. I know you're doing the best you can. You'd never send me in there if you weren't doing the best you could to make sure I was taken care of. I'm just a little freaked out by everything that's happened since last night."

Taylor smiled. "I have some ideas to smooth the transition in and out a little bit. I'll get with Miranda when she gets back and show her my improvements so she can adjust her spells accordingly. I think that will work."

"Any little bit will help."

Quinn finished the last sandwich and then sat in the kitchen and checked out some videos on her phone while Taylor got back to work on her computer and the VR system.

Clark and Miranda were gone until well into the afternoon. They finally arrived back with a full load of groceries that should hold them over for the next week or so. Clark liked to limit their trips to the small shopping center a few miles away just in case they were accidentally spotted by someone they knew. Any mention of them, even on social media, could pinpoint their location for the VirSync slayer teams.

Quinn helped put things away, and with her assistance, Clark made an early dinner as it got dark outside. He started a homemade marinara sauce with chopped onions, crushed tomatoes, a variety of seasonings, and some ground beef he'd first browned in a pan.

When he offered a taste to Quinn, her eyes rolled back in her head, and she said, "Mmmm, that is amazing. I never knew it was so simple to make."

Cooking food, to her, consisted of heating prepared meals in a microwave, not making things from scratch. Growing up, she'd never had anyone take any time with her to show her how to cook.

While Clark finished up, she set the small round table in the kitchen. A few minutes later, the four of them sat down to eat the spaghetti dinner Clark had prepared. They'd been eating for about fifteen minutes when a chime sounded from Taylor's computer in the dining room.

"That's the alert that they've fired up their VR system again." Taylor hopped up and went to check her message.

Clark shook his head as he slid his chair back and stood. "It can't be good news if they've acquired another target this soon after last night's failed mission."

Miranda turned to Quinn. "Are you up to going back in again so soon?"

"I'm good. Hell, I'm better than good since I juiced up this afternoon."

"Quinn," Miranda said, "you can never do that again. Do you understand?"

"I mean, I don't plan on it, but I survived, so what's the big deal?"

"That sort of thing causes issues with the flow of magic over a whole region. It could draw unwanted attention if the wrong people notice."

"You don't think…"

"It only lasted a few seconds. I don't think there was time enough to localize it, but I definitely felt it here. Even Taylor sensed something, and she's no spell caster. If it were to happen again, I think those sensitive to such things would try to find the source of the disturbance."

Quinn ran upstairs and quickly changed into her huntress gear. She was glad she hadn't caused anyone else any problems when she jacked into the power of the ley line.

By the time she was back downstairs a few minutes later, Taylor and Miranda had everything ready to go.

"Where are you sending me this time? Back to the city?"

Taylor shook her head without looking up from the triple screens. "I'm not sure. Everything is scrambled. I think they might suspect how we found them, and now they're trying to cover their tracks."

Clark grumbled from behind Taylor's chair, "They're going after Filippa again. That's got to be it. I warned her to remain here, but she had to do things her own way, as usual. This time, I'll make sure she listens."

Quinn climbed onto the table and settled the VR headset over her head. She spotted new runes scribed on the metal and leather of the headband. Miranda and Taylor must've upgraded the gear with healing runes like they'd said they would.

"Ready?" Miranda asked her.

"Yeah, let's do this. The sooner I get out there, the sooner I can track down where they are and call Clark." Quinn reached up and tapped the side of her face to make sure the earpiece was secure.

"On my mark," Taylor said. "Three, two, one...mark!"

Quinn once again had a sudden spinning sensation and nausea, although it wasn't as strong as before. While it was better, even a little nausea was uncomfortable. The headache came back with a vengeance, too. She squinted as she stared into the VR goggles, then the spinning increased, and she fell into blackness.

The trip was shorter this time. Quinn opened her eyes in the middle of a cluster of trees somewhere. She retched and bent over, once again emptying her stomach contents on the ground.

Quinn stood up and looked around to get her bearings. There were no landmarks to zero in on here in the woods like this. She spotted a full moon through the tree branches. Bringing up the HUD map, Quinn tried to figure out where she was, and after expanding the map outward, she saw streets and roads bordering a broad blank space that must be the wooded area in which she stood.

She shook her head. That was still no help. Quinn expanded the map a little more and checked for the red dots of slayers nearby. She finally found them, and judging from the amount of zooming out she had to do, they were a good distance away.

There were no road or place names on the map, so she

had no idea where she was. Better wait to call Clark until she had some idea of where they were. She took off through the woods in the direction of the six red dots moving slowly across the map.

She dialed up her stamina bar and drew on it to increase her speed. She was surprised by how little her stamina status changed this time. Her recharge earlier had given her a lot of power to draw upon. Quinn picked up speed until she raced through the trees, weaving in and out of them in a dark blur of motion. There was no way to tell how close the slayers were to their final target, whoever it was.

Quinn opened her enhanced senses and tried to draw in all the scents as she ran along. The familiarity of what she sensed surprised her. The smell of the forest, the faint tang of the brackish water of the Chesapeake Bay nearby, and other things she couldn't quite identify, all seemed like things she should know.

She kept working at it in her mind as she sped through the trees, closing the gap on the slayer hit team ahead of her. She'd almost reached them when everything snapped into focus.

Recognition of the various smells and sensory input gelled when her eyes fell on something familiar in the HUD map.

Quinn froze behind a tree, knowing the slayers were probably close enough to hear her. It didn't matter. She had no time to do anything sneaky. It was an emergency.

She tapped at the earpiece and waited while she searched for signs of the slayers amidst the trees ahead.

Please let her be in time.

"Quinn, you're on speaker," Taylor said.

Quinn probably didn't need the phone. She was so close already that it didn't matter anymore. She shouted, "Guys, get out! Run!"

"Quinn, you're not making any sense. We're safe here at the farmhouse. Talk to Clark."

Quinn glanced at the HUD map. "There's no time. The target IS the farmhouse. Watch out. They're all around you!"

CHAPTER NINETEEN

Clark paced across the room and back again for the twentieth time, returning to stand beside Miranda. He stared down at the empty dining room table.

"What's taking her so long?" he asked. "She's been gone for over five minutes. She called right away last time."

Taylor pointed at the center screen with the brain scan alpha wave data streaming back to them. "She's not spiking, and everything is nice and even, although it going faster than usual. She must be running."

"We should call her," Miranda said. "After the incident today, maybe we should have figured out another way to take care of this. She needs some time to cycle the extra power out of her system. She might be tempted to do something rash."

Taylor's phone rang, and she swiped the screen to pick up. "Quinn, you're on speaker."

"Taylor, get out! Run!"

"Quinn, you're not making any sense. We're safe here at the farmhouse. Talk to Clark."

Clark started to say something, but the voice on the phone cut him off.

"There's no time. The target IS the farmhouse. Watch out. They're all around you!"

His head jerked up and he stared out the dining room's bay window at the darkness outside. He couldn't see a thing. The lights in the room were blinding his night vision.

Drawing his sword, he swung around to go turn out the lights so he could see outside and the three of them wouldn't be lit up like sitting ducks. "Get down and stay down."

Miranda shook her head and hunched over Taylor in her chair, staring at the monitors. "We have to hurry up and bring her back."

"There's no time," Clark said. "She must be close anyway. She can hit them from behind. You two take cover. I'll come back and get you when we're finished."

Taylor started furiously tapping on the keyboard. "We can't take the chance that she gets caught in there. We don't know what will happen if we can't bring her back."

"I don't understand," Clark said, stopping halfway to the light. "Why can't she just walk back if she's that close?"

"Because she's not *all* there," Miranda said as she started pulling out spell components and setting them on the table where Quinn had been lying. "Part of her essence remains here in the computer system while she's out there. It has something to do with how the programming allows her to access new skills and talents while she's inside. If the computer shuts down without bringing her back, I'm afraid it'll kill her or worse."

Clark didn't want to know what was worse in this situation. "Fine, get her back. I'm still shutting the lights off. Watch your backs."

He turned back around and reached for the switch, but he didn't make it. The bay window burst inward in a shower of glass and wood as three black-clad figures with glowing red eyes leaped into the room.

"Get back!" he called as he charged forward, flinging a throwing knife at a slayer holding a crossbow leveled at Miranda's back. The knife missed the slayer but struck the stock of the crossbow, knocking the shot wide. The bolt flew across the room to lodge in the wall.

Clark followed up by jumping up so he slid across the dining room table. He swung his right leg around to kick the slayer in the head.

The slayer's glowing red eyes rolled up in his head, and he dropped to the floor.

Clark landed in a crouch beside him and brought his sword down through the center of the slayer's chest.

He didn't wait to make sure that one was dead. The other two slayers who'd dived through the window had started toward Miranda and Taylor.

Miranda had cast some sort of shield between her, the tech witch, and the advancing attackers.

Two more crossbow bolts flew at the women. The hastily erected invisible barrier worked, causing the bolts to clatter to the floor.

The attackers drew medieval longswords and charged, angling slightly away from the two women.

At first, their movements confused Clark. He thought they must be trying to circumvent Miranda's barrier. Then one brought her sword crashing down on the first of the computer monitors arrayed on the tabletop.

Taylor shouted, "They're trying to destroy the VR rig. Stop them!"

Clark understood then the attack wasn't just about killing the hunter team. It was about eliminating their ability to cause further interference.

He shifted direction toward the woman smashing at the monitors. She'd destroyed the first one and lifted her sword to strike the second. Clark pushed his hunter strength and speed to its limits. He blocked the downward blow, deflecting the sword to the side so it hacked into the table beside the two remaining monitors.

The slayer turned to face him, her face locked in an angry grimace. "You can't stop us, Hunter. You're taking on more enemies than you can fathom."

Clark ducked under the slayer's counterattack and lunged to try to get past her guard with a thrust at her gut. "I've faced impossible odds before. I've survived this long, haven't I?"

He punctuated his words with a grunt as he pushed the blade home. Before the woman danced backward, he managed to score a hit on her stomach, slashing open the fabric of the black shirt and cutting deep into her belly. Black ichor oozed from the wound, not blood.

The woman clutched at the wound with her free hand and moved her blade to use its superior length to advantage over Clark's short sword.

She blocked the first two followup attacks but missed the third.

Clark's shouted, "Ah-ha!" followed his finding the angle

to break through her defense. His blade bit deep into the woman's neck, almost decapitating her.

As this opponent dropped to the floor, Clark turned to the third slayer. That one was facing away from the hunter. He had both Taylor and Miranda clinging to his back, trying to pull him away from the computer system.

The male slayer had started to cut through one of the multiple cable bundles with his sword, a Japanese katana. He ignored the two women on his back, trying again and again to cut at the wires leading into the rear of the computer tower beneath the dining room table.

Clark dove and hacked down at the slayer's sword hand. His blessed silver blade cut cleanly through flesh and bone, severing the arm at the elbow.

At the same time, Taylor raised her arm, another of Clark's throwing knives in her hand. He hadn't given her another one, so she must have helped herself to his arsenal chest in the basement. He'd deal with that later.

Taylor's arm came down three times, stabbing the slayer's back before the man fell to his knees and toppled forward. A few seconds later, he ceased struggling beneath the two women.

Clark rose to a crouch, staying low in case any attackers outside had crossbows. "You both unhurt?"

Miranda nodded and Taylor said, "I'm good."

Clark pointed at the computer gear. "Is it still working? Can we get her back?"

Taylor nodded as she glanced at the remaining two working monitors. "I think so. I have to splice some wires, and it'll take me a few minutes.

The faint clash of steel on steel outside drew his attention. "Do what you can here, kid. Miranda, cast a barrier across the window after I leave, and watch Taylor's back."

"Where are you going?" Miranda asked.

"I hear Quinn fighting outside. She'll need help. As soon as you're ready, bring her back. Don't wait for the call, just run the recall sequence."

Taylor had already started examining the cut wires beneath the table and didn't respond to him.

Miranda said. "Don't worry, we'll take care of it."

Clark didn't wait any longer. He stood and took two steps before leaping through the window into the darkness. He landed in the grass, got his bearings, and darted to the left toward the sounds of fighting.

CHAPTER TWENTY

Quinn raced through the trees, feeling surer of herself now that she knew where she was. She also knew what the stakes were. Three of the six red dots in the HUD moved into the farmhouse. The other three fanned out to form an arc around this side of the building.

She angled for the closest of the dots while she drew on her amulet to enhance her night vision. She muttered the activation phrase she'd created: "Dammit, I need to see."

The hazy black and white before her eyes gained sharpness and definition in the bright moonlight.

Quinn spotted the slayer and raced forward at full speed, her Bowie raised to strike at the figure's back.

The man must've heard her coming because he turned. He brought around a crossbow that had been hidden from her before. He moved nearly as fast as she did, raising the weapon and firing at her.

Quinn juked to the left while bringing her knife down

across her body. The descending blade caught the speeding bolt in midair and deflected it away from her chest.

Not waiting to marvel at the odds of doing what she'd just done, she kicked out with her left leg to push off a tree, shifting direction to target the slayer who'd fired at her.

The man had dropped the crossbow and drawn a pair of what were either long knives or maybe short swords, holding them ready for the charging huntress.

Quinn boosted her speed even more, dropped to the ground, and slid with her legs leading the way. The move brought her in under the double attack the slayer launched at her with the blades.

Her right foot kicked the legs out from under the slayer, dropping him to the ground on his side.

Quinn used her remaining momentum to dig into the ground with her left foot and pop her back to her feet beside the downed opponent. The glowing red eyes flashed with a brief moment of fear just before she thrust her Bowie into his neck.

He jerked once beneath her blade, then was still as the light dimmed from the staring eyes.

Quinn moved to cover behind a nearby tree, where she crouched and searched for the next slayer in the arc outside the farmhouse. Her enhanced hearing picked up the shouts of a struggle inside.

She shook her head, Clark and the others would have to deal with that for now. Quinn cleared her thoughts to focus on the targets out here. She had to trust Clark to protect Taylor and Miranda.

A check of the HUD revealed the next closest slayer outside the home had shifted his position and started in

Quinn's direction. She concentrated while she whispered, "Mist" and smiled as the hazy blur around the edges of her vision signified that she'd dropped into shadow and was hidden from view.

Quinn waited ten long seconds, made more anxious at hearing more shouts from inside the farmhouse.

Her patience was rewarded. The slayer who'd started her way came into view, darting from tree to tree. He stopped occasionally and looked around. She was sure he was searching for his missing comrade.

Quinn shifted around to the other side of the tree so she could move behind the approaching slayer.

She moved carefully to the next tree in her line of movement. Her ability to hide in the shadows wasn't perfect invisibility. If he looked right at her, especially outlined against the light coming from the house at her back, the slayer would surely see her.

A few more careful moves, working to remain silent, put Quinn behind the slayer, about ten yards away. He was almost to the place where his companion lay dead on the ground. This slayer also carried a crossbow.

She lined up her angle of attack and darted out from behind a tree, charging at his back with her Bowie raised to strike.

He detected her approach. The slayer spun around, snapping off a shot with his crossbow.

Quinn slashed downward with her blade but wasn't so lucky this time. She gasped in pain and tumbled to the ground when the speeding bolt slammed into her left thigh. The powerful blow knocked her leg out from beneath her, sending her tumbling to the ground.

She fought through the pain and turned her fall into a rolling dive. It wasn't perfect, but she managed to come up to a kneeling position with her Bowie raised to deflect the next attack she knew had to be coming.

The slayer swung a medieval longsword down in a slashing attack at her from above.

Quinn caught the attack with her knife and twisted her arm to the side to deflect the powerful blow into the forest floor beside her.

Twisting with the incoming attack, she summoned more strength, punching up into the slayer's gut with enough force to launch him back several feet. He stumbled but managed to keep himself upright.

The break in the action was enough to allow her to climb back to her feet. Her injured leg nearly buckled again from the pain. A quick glance down at her leg spotted the feathered end of the crossbow bolt sticking out of her thigh a few inches above her knee. The leg throbbed, and she tested it by putting more weight on it. It held, but she was at nowhere near a hundred percent.

The slayer opposite her showed his teeth in an unfriendly grin. He knew she was injured and would likely try to take advantage by forcing her to push off that side. That's what she would do in this situation.

Two could play that game, though. Clark had told her in a fight to the death, making assumptions could kill you. Quinn ground her teeth together against the pain as she feinted right and then darted to the left despite her injury to get around the guy. It pushed her injured leg to its limit.

Her opponent's eyes widened in surprise at her move. He'd already started to react to the feint.

Quinn took advantage of it, driving in hard while he tried to twist to meet the attack that had caught him off-balance.

He managed to bring his sword around in a half-strength slash at her face. It was an attempt to distract her into bringing the Bowie knife up to parry it and give him the time he needed to recover.

Quinn opted to twist her upper body to the side so even more weight rested atop the injured leg. Agony flared as it started to give out at last and her vision tunneled as a result of the pain. She fought through it and turned her pending collapse into a desperate attack.

Quinn drove ahead with her shoulder, taking the slayer in the side of his ribs beneath his raised arm.

At the same time, she pulled her Bowie around in a broad arc and plunged it into the guy's back just beneath the ribs, slicing into his kidney and eliciting a scream of pain as his free hand reached back to try to grasp the hand holding the knife in his back.

Quinn yanked the blade free and fell to her side.

The slayer stumbled to the side, too, as the mortal injury registered. He fell to his knees and then slumped over to the side, his face inches from Quinn's.

She watched to be sure the red glow in the eyes began to fade before she turned to get back to her feet and search for another target.

Quinn rose to one knee to start looking for the remaining slayer out here with her. Her injured leg had finally given out, and her free hand clutched at the stub of the crossbow bolt still protruding from the wound.

She spared a moment to glance down at her leg, then

tightened her grip on the shaft while she tried to decide whether to try to pull it out. She didn't know what to do.

"If you pull it out, you'll likely cut open your artery, if it's not cut already. Then I wouldn't have the joy of killing you myself."

Quinn looked around for the source of the familiar voice.

Cindy, her eyes glowing bright red, stepped from behind a nearby tree. She had a crossbow leveled at Quinn's chest as she moved forward. "You fell right into our trap. It took us a while to figure out who had killed our brethren at the fae's home and then got away without being seen by any of the others. Once we realized how, it was easy to figure out who. Myles sends his regards. He would ordinarily offer to hire you and whoever managed the technical wizardry needed to pull this off, but in this situation, he was sure you would turn us down."

"He was right. There's no way we're switching sides."

"Really? You can't win. We hold all the power, all the resources. Why not join us? We can conjure up an endless army of creatures and demons to fight you. We can lose as many as it takes. You can only lose once."

Quinn had to keep her talking and hope the others were faring better inside. "That's exactly why you'll lose. You claim it's your strength, but it's your biggest weakness. You use people up and throw them away like trash when it suits you. Eventually, your minions catch on and change sides."

Cindy laughed. "You think fighting for the light is any different? You're just a pawn to them."

Quinn remembered something Miranda had said

earlier. "Yes, but I don't fight for either side. I fight for balance. Light and dark are just two sides of the same thing, aren't they? I, on the other hand, fight for all the gray in the middle. That's where I'll make my stand."

Cindy's eyes flashed in annoyance at Quinn's answer.

The demon-kinder's reaction offered only a little solace, though. Quinn was getting dizzy and might pass out at any instant. The loss of blood from the injury was severe, not that she'd live long enough to die from that if Cindy had her way.

She stared at her opponent, and a strange thought crossed through her mind. Quinn forced herself to focus through the dizziness on the demon-kinder's hands. She wore dark leather gloves on both of them.

"Hey, didn't I cut your hand off the last time we saw each other?"

Cindy laughed. "You puny humans are so fragile. I can't imagine how your kind has survived in this world for so long. It took me a great deal of personal energy, but I managed to force this puny body to regrow its missing appendage."

"Neat trick. You should teach it to me sometime." Quinn swayed as she said it and nearly toppled over. She reached out and steadied herself on the tree beside her. Maybe she could fall that way and roll behind cover. It would allow her to try to escape for a little while.

"I tire of this, Huntress. Know that this was the last piece of our plan. Finishing you off puts everything else is in place. You even helped us with your ham-fisted rescue the other night. It flushed out some of the others attending the fae summit. Now I think it's time to end you and then attend to your friends inside." The woman tilted her head to sight along the crossbow's stock and took aim.

Everything slowed down for Quinn. It was as if time had stopped moving at normal speed. Her eyes were hyper-focused on the finger tightening on the crossbow's trigger. At the same time, her dizziness shifted, now different from what she'd experienced from her injury.

Quinn smiled when she realized what that meant. Hopefully, it had come in time.

Ten feet away. Cindy squeezed the trigger. Quinn saw the bolt started to slide forward, propelled faster and faster as it left the bow's front edge. Time was returning to normal again.

At the same instant, blackness tugged Quinn backward. Despite the sudden onset of migraine-level pain, she welcomed the recall. She even pushed at it, trying to escape certain death.

The last thing she saw was the bolt flying straight at her chest.

CHAPTER TWENTY-ONE

Q uinn gasped and sat up. A thrumming snap next to her caused her to look down.

There, still quivering in the wooden tabletop, was a crossbow bolt.

"That was close," she said to no one in particular.

"Oh, my God, Quinn, you've got an arrow in you," Taylor exclaimed.

"Technically, it's a bolt, but yeah, I've got an arrow in me." Quinn glanced around, spotting the three dead bodies around the table. "Where's Clark?"

"He went out looking for you," Miranda explained. "He was worried. So were we. We had to fix things here. We just finished the repair and decided to pull you back."

Quinn glanced at the still-quivering bolt in the table beside her and smiled. "You have excellent timing."

Taylor's gaze followed hers to the feathered shaft. She shivered.

Miranda came over and helped Quinn slide to the

table's edge. "Let me take a glance at that leg. It looks nasty."

"I don't think the bone's broken, but I'm not sure how to remove it."

"Ordinarily," the witch said, "this would be a job for a surgeon. That, however, would open us up to all sorts of odd questions, so I'm going to have to work on it."

"Hold up until Clark gets back. Cindy is still out there, and she's dangerous."

"You're losing a lot of blood. You need to let me work on that leg now. Taylor, come over here and help me lay her back down on the table."

Quinn tried to resist, but it was useless; she was too weak. The two women soon had her staring at the ceiling while one of them tore open her jeans around the wound.

"Hold her down," Miranda ordered.

Taylor came around to stand beside Quinn. Her friend gave her half a smile and leaned over to grip the injured leg.

Miranda grabbed her leg with one hand and the stub of the bolt with the other, then muttered some words Quinn didn't recognize under her breath. It must have been some sort of magic because Quinn's amulet grew colder for a few seconds.

The witch tensed her shoulder muscles, and Quinn prepared for the coming pain. A pulling sensation yanked several times at her leg, jerking and tugging. There wasn't any pain, however.

After a few seconds, Miranda sighed and stood upright, holding the bloody bolt in one hand. "Taylor, jam as much of that gauze into the wound as you can to stop the bleeding. Just stuff it in there using your fingers until you can't fit any more or the bleeding stops."

She turned to Quinn while Taylor worked on the wound. "It was stuck in the bone, but it doesn't appear to have broken it. You're tough, I guess."

"Just good huntress genes," Quinn murmured. Her words slurred, and she had trouble keeping her eyes open.

"Quinn!" Miranda leaned over Quinn's face, holding it in both hands. "You need to stay awake until your hunter healing kicks in."

Her attempt to correct Miranda came out as an almost unintelligible jumble of syllables.

"Miranda, what's wrong with her? I stopped the bleeding like you said."

"I don't know. She should be getting better once we removed the bolt. Unless…"

Miranda turned away, moving out of from Quinn's narrowing field of view. She was really having trouble keeping her eyes open. It was almost as if she'd been…

"Drugged," Miranda announced. "They did something to these bolts, probably some sort of poison. Taylor, go up to my room and bring my big shoulder bag down. There are things I need in there."

Miranda's face came back into view, although the huntress had trouble keeping it in focus.

"Quinn, I think they poisoned the crossbow bolts. I'm going to try to counter it magically, but to do that, you need to stay awake so I can see what's working. Got that?"

Quinn's attempt at the word "yes" simply came out as a single long hissing sound. She'd lost the ability to do anything as her entire body rebelled against itself. Her eyes remained open only because she couldn't command the muscles to close them fully.

Figures and shapes moved in and out of view. Quinn wasn't sure all of them were real. After a while, she thought she picked up Clark's voice asking about her. Then her ears stopped working, and though she hadn't closed her eyes, everything faded to black silence.

She wasn't sure how long she slept or if being unconscious even counted as sleep. Quinn's eyes fluttered open to bright sunlight streaming through the window of her room at the farmhouse.

Sitting up, Quinn lifted the blankets to check out her leg. There was a large bandage covering the wounded area, which looked clean. There was no blood seeping through it. She probed the dressing with her fingers to see how tender it was. There was just an ache, and that appeared only when she pressed down hard.

Quinn folded back the covers and sat on the edge of the bed. She wore panties and a t-shirt. She stood, waiting to make sure her leg would bear her weight. It felt fine, with only a slight twinge to tell her anything had been wrong. It looked like her crazy-fast healing ability was still in play.

Crossing to her dresser, she pulled out a pair of jeans and slipped them on, followed by a fresh shirt. She turned to check out herself in the mirror behind the door. Someone had brushed her hair and French-braided it while she was out, probably Taylor. She loved that kind of thing.

Quinn slid her feet into a pair of brown knee-high boots and left to go downstairs. Voices in the kitchen drew her that way, and she entered to find Clark, Miranda, and Taylor in the midst of a lively conversation.

"Clark, you can get angry if you want," Taylor said. "All I can tell you is the truth. They destroyed enough of the system that we're significantly limited in how far I can project Quinn in VR mode. I wouldn't trust it anymore for much beyond a mile from our location."

"You said you didn't know for sure," Clark replied.

"I don't have to. I built safeties and redundancies into the system as I assembled it. I might be able to push the radius out some, but it'll take more time and equipment to get it back to full strength."

Clark threw his hands in the air. "Great, and we still don't know how they found our location."

"Filippa or one of her people could've let it slip to someone," Taylor suggested. "She's been here and would know how to direct someone to come back."

"I thought you trusted the fae woman?" Miranda asked Clark and he nodded in response.

"I do, mostly, but not everyone she shares information with is trustworthy. Our secret is only as good the least reliable link in the chain. That's why we're packing to move to a new location."

Quinn cleared her throat from the doorway. Everyone's head swiveled around in her direction.

"Quinn, what are you doing up and out of bed?" Miranda asked.

"I woke up, and I feel fine. What else would I do?"

Miranda came over and stared at her leg for a few seconds. Quinn almost felt her deciding if she could order

Quinn to let her take a look at the injury. She had to head that line of thought off right now.

"I checked the wound, and it's pretty much healed. I could've taken the bandage off, but I decided to leave it for one more day. I have super huntress healing, after all," Quinn added.

Miranda looked doubtful, but Quinn gently pushed past her and went to the table where Clark and Taylor sat.

"What's our plan now that they know where we are, and that we can fight them on their own turf inside the VR?"

Clark shook his head. "We don't have one because we can't turn our system back on now that VirSync knows how to chase us down."

"But we can't give up. Something Cindy said right before she shot me last night is bothering me."

Taylor laughed. "Quinn, it wasn't last night, it was three nights ago. You've been out since we took the bolt out of your leg and discovered the poison…"

Clark waved his hand to stop Taylor from continuing. "Quinn, what did Cindy say that bothered you?"

"She said something about their plan already being in place. She also said our rescue of Filippa and Alistair ended up helping them."

Miranda shook her head. "That doesn't sound good. We don't have the VR rig ready yet. The alert system is still working, though, right?"

Taylor nodded. "Nothing has come in since the attack. I pinged the signal interrupter to make sure it was still active and got the correct confirmation message back. They haven't used the VR at all except to attack us here."

Quinn walked over to the sink and stared out the window at the yard outside the farmhouse. "She seemed awfully smug, as if their plan was ready or had already started." She turned to face the others. "I think we have to get everyone together and find out where this fae summit is taking place. Once we do that and get close enough, we can get Taylor to try to see if the VR setup is working nearby. Then we'll know if they've infiltrated the place."

"Filippa said they'd begin the summit by the end of the week," Clark told them. "That'd be about now. She was supposed to contact me to let me know when and where in case I found out about any threats to them. She never did, which I assumed meant she didn't want our help."

"Clark," Miranda asked. "Is there any place in the city an event like this would be held so it could be kept a secret?"

"There are more than a few places. Maybe as many as a dozen that possess the necessary proximity to a nexus of ley lines. Taylor, can you detect the use of the VR tech if we get close enough, assuming they've found a way to mask it from the bot you installed?"

"Yeah, but I would need to be pretty close. Maybe as little as a hundred yards or so."

"It'll have to do," Clark said. "Let's load up. Miranda, you can drive. I'll ride shotgun. Taylor, you ride in the back and get your detection gear ready."

Quinn stopped them as they all started to leave the kitchen. "What about me?"

"What about you?" Clark said.

"You're not leaving me here. You're going to need me."

"You've been confined to bed for three days after nearly dying."

"Clark, look at me. I woke up because I'm healed. Huntress genes, remember?"

The old hunter stared at Quinn for almost five seconds before he nodded. "Gear up. This could get bad, so bring your A-game. I don't like how this is shaking out."

Quinn resisted the urge to jump up and down and pump her fist, but she couldn't stop the broad grin on her face as she raced upstairs to get her Bowie and to change into her huntress garb.

The hunt was on.

CHAPTER TWENTY-TWO

Quinn sighed. They'd been out for hours, scouring the city with no luck. The first nine places Clark checked out were all busts. They detected nothing supernatural going on with Taylor's computer rig, Miranda's magic, and Clark's and Quinn's hunter senses.

The most recent one had seemed promising at first. Quinn had smelled something akin to the shifters they'd run into in the dark alley the previous week.

When she pointed it out to Clark, he was doubtful. After sniffing the air where Quinn had detected the scent, he said, "Not strong enough for a whole pack. More than likely, it was a loner or drifter passing through."

He still took the extra time to have the team search the abandoned building. In the end, they discovered a few teenaged werewolves marking their territory the old-fashioned way on the building's fourth floor. When Quinn walked in on them peeing their initials on the dusty concrete, all three of them zipped up so fast Clark laughed aloud when one of them doubled over.

The three boys took off before they could answer any questions. Quinn and Clark returned to the car, both chuckling. When Miranda and Taylor asked what was so funny, Clark left it to Quinn to explain while they drove to the next place on his list. The three women were in stitches, laughing and sharing a rash of bad puns.

Clark cut them off as he turned down onto an old cobblestone road that dated back to Baltimore's earliest days. "Let's get back to business, ladies. We're almost to the next location."

"What is it?" Quinn asked. Having grown up in the city and spent part of her time on the streets, she'd thought she knew all the ins and outs of the place. After seeing some of the more remote places Clark had taken them today, Quinn realized she didn't know as much as she'd thought.

"This part of the city used to host lodging houses for sailors in port waiting for another berth on a merchantman getting ready to leave the harbor. It's mostly abandoned warehouses now, but there are some old places hidden in this area, most of them underground."

"What makes you think this might be the place they'd hold the summit?" Miranda asked.

"Filippa is old. Ancient, even. She mentioned the area in passing when she visited once. She convinced me to drive her over here and regaled me with incredible stories about what she called the old days."

Clark drove down a long rough-paved street. It was well after dark at this point, and there was no other traffic around them. The only other vehicles they saw were old and obviously abandoned.

"There was one spot she said was a favorite hangout for

fae visitors." Clark craned his neck over the steering wheel to see out the windshield better. "I just can't seem to remember exactly where it was."

"Stop," Taylor called from the back seat. "I've got something."

Clark halted the car and turned to Taylor, waiting for more from the tech witch.

She clicked her laptop and then picked it up, twisting in her seat while staring at the screen as if trying to pick up a cell signal on her phone. She noticed the other three watching her and smiled. "I modified the wi-fi antenna in my laptop to detect energy in the magical spectrum using a code modification I found in the VR system programing. I never thought I'd get to use it, or that it would even work. Well, it works, and I've picked up something."

Quinn caught a glimpse of the screen while Taylor moved the laptop around. An enlarged wi-fi signal triangle showed on the screen, with the lowest bar flickering on and off. "Are you sure you're not just picking up someone's local wi-fi nearby?"

"Look around, Quinn," Taylor said. "You think anybody has bothered running cable or internet down here? It looks like they barely have electricity."

Quinn shrugged as she looked at the darkened buildings outside the car. "So, which way is it?"

"Let me try something else." Taylor dug in her backpack and pulled out a computer cable to which she'd attached a broad, flat paddle fashioned from aluminum foil. "My grandfather told me a story once about how they used to make their old TV antennas work better with tinfoil. Let's see if it still applies."

Clark rolled his eyes but didn't say anything. Instead, he went back to scanning the nearby buildings from the front seat.

The instant Taylor plugged in the makeshift antenna, the wi-fi signal bars filled halfway, and the flickering of the signal stopped. She beamed at them and then looked back at the screen as she extended her arm out the rear window and slowly turned the foil paddle.

The bars peaked to full strength, then dropped away to half as she moved it.

"Taylor?" Quinn prompted.

"I saw it. Give me a sec." Taylor reversed direction and slowly passed the foil back and forth, watching the signal bars. She stopped at the same time Clark, who'd been paying no attention to them, pointed out his window.

"There," the two echoed in unison.

Quinn ducked her head to see out the windshield. They both pointed at an old stone-walled warehouse. She stared at it and then at the other buildings on either side. It didn't look any different from any other structure around them.

Clark was sure, though, as was Taylor. He shut off the car and climbed out. Taylor was already standing behind the trunk, setting the laptop on the lid. She slid her arms into her backpack straps and settled it on her back.

As Taylor stood there getting ready for what came next, Quinn noticed not one, but two sheathed throwing knives clipped to her belt. She wondered if Miranda was armed, too. It probably wasn't a bad idea.

Taylor picked up the open laptop and the paddle gadget and started walking down the darkened street. Clark walked a few feet ahead of her, running his fingers over the dark stones that made up the exterior wall of the warehouse.

He stopped by a large wooden sliding door that moved on a rail, mounted just under the roof above them. Thick chains held the door shut with a heavy-duty steel padlock.

Judging from the rust on both the links and the lock, Quinn thought it hadn't been opened in a while. "I don't think anyone has used this in a very long time, Clark."

"I don't know..." He trailed off, his voice sort of faraway.

Taylor came over to stand next to Quinn. "There is definitely something magical going on in there. It's strong, too. Off the charts, if I had charts to measure against, that is."

Quinn looked around. "Fine, how do we get in? Can you magic open the lock?"

"No," Miranda said. "It's warded. You can't detect it until you're right on top of it. It's so out of the way, you'd have to stumble on it by accident to detect it."

"Unless you knew it was a fae hangout once upon a time," Quinn said. She looked at Clark and said, "Good work, Hunter-man."

He nodded, still working on the problem of how to get inside. He took two steps back, scanning the side of the building until he pointed to a partially opened window in the wall about fifteen feet up. The window tilted around a pivot in the center and slanted out when opened.

Quinn shook her head as she stared up at it. "How do you propose to get up there?"

"I don't. I think I can get you up there, though. Once you're inside, you can help the rest of us in. There must be an entrance in there that's hidden from the outside. Locate it, and we'll come in and join you."

"Even with a boost, you can't lift me high enough to reach that window."

"Ye of little faith. Watch."

Clark returned to the car and pulled it up next to the building until he was directly beneath the window. He got out and gestured for the others to come over.

"See?"

"I see." Quinn shook her head. "I still don't like it. I'll be trapped in there with whatever is creating all the shielded magic."

"That means you'll have to hurry and find a way to let us in. You'll be fine. The fae aren't blood-thirsty. If you tell them why you're here, they'll help you let us in."

"What if the fae aren't in there and the slayers are?" Quinn asked.

Clark stared at her, and she realized she was just making excuses. She gestured to him to lead on. He climbed up to stand on the roof of the car and waited for Quinn to join him. He bent over, cupping his hands, and boosted her up until she was just below the window.

Quinn stretched but couldn't quite get her fingers high enough. "I can't reach. I need a little more."

Clark grunted, and Quinn rose a few more inches until she could just curl her fingers over the sill. Drawing on her inner strength, she pulled herself up until she managed to get her belly over the edge of the window, then slid through the narrow opening.

A wooden catwalk stretched around the upper part of the warehouse's interior. Quinn crouched and looked around, getting her bearings. She noted the increased chill from her amulet right away, warning of magic in play and potential danger. It was also too dark to see anything in here. That gave her two things she needed to do before she started searching the building.

Whispering, she said, "Dammit, I need to see." She followed it with the word, "Mist."

Now both hidden from view and able to see in the dark, Quinn scanned the inside of the warehouse. There was some sort of an opening in the wall about forty feet down to her right. It might be a door, or just an alcove in the bricks. It was on the end opposite the padlocked sliding door outside. Better try that new option first. She started down the catwalk to get a look.

A ladder extended to the floor where the catwalk turned the corner ahead. Quinn checked the rest of the empty warehouse from her vantage point and decided she'd be able to conduct a better search from the main floor.

The hairs on the back of her neck stood on end all of a sudden. Quinn froze, trying to extend her senses outward to figure out what had just happened. The warehouse still appeared to be empty as she scanned the floor below. There was nothing there, but *something* had tweaked her newly awakened huntress senses.

Drawing a deep breath, she caught the scent of baking bread and peppermint. There were fae here or very close.

Moving over to the ladder, Quinn descended to the dirt floor below. She stayed near the stone wall that bordered the street and doubled back to the darkened alcove she'd spotted from above. Whatever it was, her night vision ability couldn't penetrate the shadows there. There had to be some sort of masking spell covering whatever was in there.

She tiptoed along the stone wall and had almost reached it when something tapped her on the shoulder.

Quinn spun, drawing her Bowie in a single fluid motion, and froze when she saw the three tall figures in black cloaks and hoods holding rapiers with razor-sharp tips an inch from her neck.

A fourth cloaked figure stepped forward and said, "Miss Quinn, you should not be here."

He reached up and lowered his hood. It was the fae butler, Alistair.

Quinn held out her empty hand, making sure to hold her knife hand perfectly still. "Al, old pal, how are you doing?"

"It's Alistair, please, and I'm well. Are you alone, or did you bring Master Clark and the other members of your odd little group?"

Quinn couldn't help herself. Her eyes darted to the alcove, then back at the old man.

"I see." He sighed and turned to one of his companions. "There are three others outside. Go and fetch them in before they draw unwanted attention."

Quinn expected the guard to whom he gave the order to go check it out. To her amazement, the guard performed a complex hand signal, and four more cloaked figures materialized behind Alistair and walked past Quinn to the alcove. One second the four weren't there, then it was as if they'd stepped through a veil and appeared before her.

"Can you tell your guys here to lower their blades? I'm a friend."

"That remains to be seen," the figure closest to her muttered.

Alistair waved a hand and they lowered their swords, including the one who'd spoken.

"Thanks." Quinn sheathed her knife and walked over to where Alistair stood just outside the alcove. He was watching the impenetrable shadows in the nook as if waiting for something.

A few seconds later, Clark came through, followed by Taylor, then Miranda. The four cloaked guards came back inside last.

Clark walked over and said, "Alistair, I must see your mistress. It's very urgent."

"She told us she was not to be disturbed until she calls us."

"Alistair, you know I wouldn't come here if it wasn't important."

"I know nothing of the sort. It is true you have no true business here. This is a fae summit. Humans are admitted by invitation only."

Quinn was tired of his resistance. "Al, you don't understand. There are more of those demon-kinder out there somewhere, and they're looking for your little gathering here." Quinn gestured at the cloaked figures, then stood with her hands on her hips. "You've got all these burly he-men with swords around, but they're not going to mean much when it comes to fighting off a bunch of enraged demon-kinder with superhuman strength. It takes a woman's wiles and craftiness to make sure you're safe."

Alistair sighed and waved his hand.

All seven of the cloaked guards lowered their hoods.

Quinn gawked at the seven tall, thin fae women.

Taylor laughed. "That'll teach you to generalize, Quinn."

Clark held up his hand to halt the chatter and turned back to Alistair. "We're here now. You might as well invite us in until Filippa wakes up or comes out from wherever she has sequestered herself. I need to speak to her as soon as she does."

Alistair nodded. "Very well. Come with me. I must caution you to keep your hands to yourself. Don't touch anything. Follow."

Quinn fell in behind Clark, who followed the old man. Taylor and Miranda were behind Quinn. The four of them walked with the fae butler toward the center of the warehouse and that which had been hidden.

CHAPTER TWENTY-THREE

Quinn and the others followed Alistair. The guards flanked them, three on either side and one walking behind. She wasn't sure what the old man had planned since the warehouse was clearly empty. There must be a secret basement or something.

Something wasn't right. The building wasn't empty, not even close.

One second, Quinn walked through an empty warehouse, and the next, she passed between a pair of striped round pavilions to enter the middle of a broad circle, with seven huge tents in all.

She looked back over her shoulder at the warehouse's corner. She could still see the rest of the warehouse as if nothing had changed. From this angle, it looked normal. The only difference was now the center had a small encampment of elves in the middle of it.

A voice behind her said, "We are fae, *not* elves, thank you."

Quinn turned to confront a tall woman wearing a long, flowing white gown and a sort of turban.

"Hey, were you just in my head?"

"You humans," the woman said with a wave of her hand. "Your thoughts are front and center all the time. It's like you're shouting at everyone wherever you go. I couldn't stop listening to your thoughts if I wanted to."

"That's just rude. You need to apologize."

Clark appeared at Quinn's side and placed a hand on her shoulder. The iron grip he applied made her stand down. He offered the woman a deep bow. "My apologies, Princess. She's my ward, and I have failed to impress upon her the importance of proper decorum."

Quinn started to complain; she was not his ward. He shifted his boot and stepped on her foot hard enough to cause pain. She bit back a yelp and turned to glare at him. She got the hint, though, and closed her mouth.

The woman inclined her head at Clark. "I accept your apology, Hunter. My cousin has told me all about you. My condolences on the loss of your clan."

"I thank you. The pain and loss have faded some. It was almost twenty years ago now."

"That's right. I forget how short-lived you people are. To me, twenty years is but the blink of an eye."

Quinn shifted her boot, and it slid out from under Clark's foot. "I'm sorry, too, Princess. I had no idea my thoughts would be so transparent to you. You mentioned your cousin. I assume you mean Filippa?"

Clark jumped in. "Yes, Princess Carina here is a member of one of the seven fae royal houses. Filippa belongs to another of them."

Carina's expression changed to disinterested amusement. "I call her a cousin, but it's a case of kinship of station, rather than blood, although I suppose there is a bit of that as well."

"Princess Carina comes from the Indian subcontinent. Each of the royal families represents a different part of the world."

Quinn examined all the tents. The stripes and patterns presented a variety of colors and designs. She figured each one identified the royal houses and the region from which they came. The pavilions' colors carried over into the outfits of the fae passing in and out of them. There was a great deal of bustle and activity around all the tents except one.

Nodding to the single inactive tent, Quinn asked, "Is that one empty? Are you still waiting for one of your number to arrive?"

Carina tipped her head toward the tent, then looked away as if dismissing it. "That is Filippa's. She sent word that she is ill. She's in there, or at least she was. We all saw her arrive, but she's keeping all her people in with her, except for Alistair here." The princess turned to the Fae butler. "You must tell her we tire of her dramatics. If she is really ill, I or another of the royals possesses enough healing power to take care of any malady."

"I will pass along your message," Alistair said, shifting back and forth on his feet and shooting a brief glance at his faction's pavilion.

Quinn glanced that way again. For a moment, the entrance wavered, shimmering like the air over asphalt on a hot day. Her amulet grew cold for an instant, then warmed again. She absently stroked at the pendant with her fingertips for a few seconds. The shimmering effect had stopped, and she tried to understand what she'd just seen and felt.

Clark nudged her with his elbow. "Quinn, the princess was addressing you."

"I'm sorry, Princess. There's so much here to distract me. When did you say Filippa and her people arrived?"

"I didn't say, but it was just this morning. That is not important, though. My question for you had to do with how someone so young finds themselves in training to become a hunter? It's been quite a long time in human years since the unfortunate demise of the clans."

"I prefer huntress, Your Highness. It speaks to my particular abilities."

"Really? And what might those be?"

Clark cut Quinn off as she started to answer. "We are still trying to ascertain exactly what my young apprentice here can do. Her training is challenging."

"Of course," Carina said. "I understand." She suddenly smiled and nodded past them. "My ill cousin has chosen to come out and see what the fuss was all about. Filippa, darling, we have some rather remarkable visitors who stumbled on our secret location. You wouldn't know anything about that, would you? They came looking for you."

Quinn turned to see Filippa and a group of tall fae men and women come from their pavilion. The amulet changed from warm to a biting chill in an instant, putting the huntress in her on edge. There was danger present. She scanned the area around the pavilions to find the source, but nothing was evident.

She glanced to her side, but Clark didn't seem to be concerned. His amulet didn't seem to work the same way hers did, though. It was one of the things that made her special.

Her hand itched to reach under her jacket and draw her Bowie, but she held off. Clark would be pissed if she caused some sort of international fae incident. The amulet's chill could be a reaction to some random and harmless fae magic nearby. Maybe.

Filippa coughed as she approached, covering her mouth with her fingers as she did. The seven attendants around her fanned out in a loose semi-circle, curving around the group at the center of the circle of tents.

Behind the newly arrived group of fae, the tent entrance shimmered again, and her amulet grew even colder. A few seconds later, even more people emerged from Filippa's pavilion. These new people moved in both directions toward the other tents.

Carina and Filippa greeted each other with a warm hug. They spoke in a language unlike any Quinn had heard before. It had a songlike quality to it.

While they chatted in Fae-ish or whatever it was, Quinn scanned the circle and noticed that two of Filippa's people now stood idly by each of the other tents. Her head whipped around at the mention of her name.

Filippa held her hands out to Quinn as she came forward. As she stretched out her arms, her billowing green sleeves rode up, baring forearms wearing that same silver bracelet on the left wrist Quinn had seen her wearing before. It must be a sign of her station. Quinn glanced at the other princess. Carina had a similar one in the shape of a fine braided rope, worn over a small tattoo of a snarling tiger.

The huntress stared at Filippa's wrist, bare except for the bracelet.

The newly arrived fae princess was close, still reaching to embrace her.

Quinn knew what she was about to do was based only on the barest of hunches. There was no time to warn Clark or the others.

If she was wrong, there would be hell to pay.

Quinn pushed off her back foot, spinning in place as she drew upon her stamina to boost her strength and reaction speed. Her booted foot came around in a perfectly executed kick, catching Filippa in the face and sending her flying backward to collide with two of her attendants. The Irish fae princess and the others collapsed in a jumble of arms and legs, trying to untangle themselves and rise again.

"Quinn, have you gone insane?" Clark clutched her arm as she landed back on her feet and reached for her Bowie.

She shook off his grip easily, her enhanced strength allowing her to pull out of his grasp. Quinn drew her blade and advanced on the tangled trio on the ground, and gasps of shock came from the fae around her.

Quinn turned to her mentor. "Clark, that's not her. It's not Filippa. Can't you see? They're all slayers."

Clark's eyes at first registered surprise and anger, but then they widened even more. Quinn caught the reflection of a flickering orange flame in them and twisted to look behind her.

The pair of fake fae at the tent behind her channeled dual torrents of magical flames from their hands at the canvas pavilion. The fire had already spread across the tent's pitched roof.

Screams echoed around them now.

"Duck!"

Quinn complied with Clark's snapped command, based on long hours of training with him over the last month. His blade thrust through the space where she'd just stood, taking the charging slayer behind her in the chest.

Quinn twisted and slid to one side, her Bowie in hand as she moved toward Filippa, only it wasn't Filippa anymore. Cindy rose from the ground, the spell or demonic disguise broken.

She wiped her mouth, which had a trickle of black fluid leaking from it. "You'll pay for that, Huntress."

"Try me. I'll knock you down again if you want."

All around Quinn, the slayers who'd come with Cindy fought with the fae guards who'd escorted Clark and his group here. It appeared many of the other real fae were either not here or trapped now in the burning tents.

Miranda's hands wove a pattern in the air while Taylor stood at her back with a silver knife in each hand. The witch spread her fingers, and what looked like a tiny gray cloud appeared. Then it started raining sideways, water spraying from the hovering cloud. She directed the magical rain shower upon the closest of the burning tents.

Quinn took all this in from the background as she and

Cindy circled each other. Each held off, looking for an opening to attack the other.

"Huntress, I'd love to know how you saw through my disguise. It fooled the Fae with ease."

"Did you think I wouldn't be able to tell you and your slayers were around? Your plan didn't allow for our presence here, did it?"

"I'll admit it did not. You forced us to execute our plan early. We will be unable to take all the fae leaders. Still, two should be enough to dissolve the mutual cooperation agreement between the royal families."

As Cindy said it, two slayers pulled a struggling Carina to Filippa's tent. Two other slayers followed and fought off the remaining guards trying to stop the kidnapping. Behind them, the shimmering entrance of the tent awaited the princess and those who took her.

They were running out of time, so Quinn charged at Cindy. It was a rash move, born of desperation, but she realized now that Cindy had been playing for time. As she ran in, she called out, "Clark, the princess."

She didn't have time to determine whether he'd heard her. Cindy had drawn a long curved dagger from her belt and slashed at the huntress as she charged in.

Quinn somehow pulled herself forward and down in time for the blade to pass over her head, missing by a fraction of an inch. She didn't know how close it had come to connecting until a two-inch lock of hair from her ponytail fell past her face.

She growled. The demon-kinder was going to pay for that.

Quinn turned her bent-over rush into a textbook

tackle, hitting Cindy's thighs with her shoulder and driving the woman backward.

As the demon-kinder stumbled away, she pulled free from Quinn's grasp.

The huntress slashed out with her knife, though, opening a gash in Cindy's thigh.

Quinn had reached a bit too far, and the move left her off-balance. She couldn't stop herself and fell forward. Trying to salvage the fall, she tucked her head into a controlled roll, hoping to end up back on her feet.

Cindy had other plans. The demon-kinder's foot snaked out from amidst the billowing pants she wore. She caught Quinn in the gut, sending her flipping and rolling across the ground.

Quinn ended up facedown. Worse yet, she'd dropped her Bowie when she was hit. She searched for her weapon as she scrambled to get back to her feet. There was no time left for mistakes. Cindy and another of the slayers ran straight at her.

Digging her toes into the warehouse's dirt floor, Quinn launched herself in a diving lunge to the side, perpendicular to Cindy's approach. It put her closer to the charging slayer, but Quinn liked her chances better against only one of them when she was still down on the ground like this.

She turned the lunge into a rolling tumble at the end, narrowly avoiding the sword belonging to the other slayer. It plunged into the dirt behind the small of her back.

While it didn't connect with Quinn, it did pin her leather jacket in place. She jerked to a stop, unable to roll any farther.

Cindy stepped forward with her dagger raised high.

Quinn pulled her arms free of the jacket just in time. Cindy's plunging blade scored a slash on Quinn's shoulders as she rolled free of the trapped coat.

This time, Quinn managed to regain her feet. She turned to face Cindy and the male slayer opposite her.

All around, fighting continued. Bodies lay everywhere. Quinn couldn't tell which was friend or foe. Two of the tents still blazed.

Unarmed, Quinn searched for anything she could use as a weapon. In desperation, she slipped off her leather shoulder rig and held it out to one side. It was the only weapon she had.

The slayer was the closest to her, and Quinn swung the leather straps in a circle over her head and then flung them at the feet of the onrushing attacker.

She laughed aloud when the desperate move actually worked. The harness tangled around the slayer's ankles. His eyes widened as he pitched forward, the longsword flying out of his hands to skid to a stop at Quinn's feet.

She stooped to pick up the weapon, ready to defend against Cindy's attack.

It never came. The woman was nowhere to be seen.

Quinn twisted around and searched for the demon-kinder, expecting to find she had gotten behind her somehow. Then she spotted the demon-kinder leader.

Cindy stood at the shimmering entrance to the tent. The few surviving slayers still in sight, including the one Quinn had tripped, ran past her and disappeared inside. As soon as the survivors passed her, the woman shot Quinn an evil grin and raised her curved dagger in salute. Then she turned and dashed into the pavilion's interior. When

Cindy vanished, the shimmering around the entrance stopped, too.

Quinn stood from her crouch, still holding the longsword as she searched around for any signs of danger. Her amulet had returned to normal, but she wanted to be sure.

Clark stood nearby, four slayer bodies arrayed around him. Taylor, still holding her silver knives, wiped her brow with the back of her hand and smiled at Quinn. The huntress noticed both blades were bloody.

Miranda walked back from the final pavilion, where she'd doused the flames at last. The way she trudged across the warehouse's dirt floor showed her magic use had drained her.

The six fae tents that had been ablaze were wrecked. Most of the high pitched roofs had burned away, leaving only a few tent poles still standing to support the canvas sides. Quinn couldn't tell if there were any injured or dead inside them.

"Alistair," Clark shouted. He stalked across the center of the tent circle toward the old man, who was standing off to one side, wringing his hands. The hunter extended his blade at the fae butler as he approached. "You had to have known. Why didn't you say something or get word to me before this?"

"I was told they'd kill her instantly if I didn't comply with their demands. They assured me they only wanted to capture the assembled princesses. The woman who disguised herself as my mistress told me no one would be harmed."

Quinn ran to Filippa's tent to look inside. It was empty,

which she expected. The shimmering had to be some sort of transporter spell like they used to send out the slayers.

"They're not here, Clark." Quinn turned to face Alistair. "Where'd they take them?"

"I do not know, Huntress. I never saw the outside of the place where they held us. It was dark in there all the time. The black drapes were kept closed so we couldn't see out the windows. It was furnished with fine old furniture of the sort the princess would have chosen back home."

Taylor came forward. "Was it all old leather couches and chairs and stuff?"

Alistair nodded, although he seemed to take issue with the description.

"I know that place. It's the vampire's lair. They're holding the two princesses prisoner in that building downtown."

Clark shook his head. "That's not good. It's going to be hard to break into it.

"Not if I can get in there first and shut off the security cameras. Then they won't see you coming," Quinn said. "Taylor, how long will it take you to get the VR rig back up and running? Can you do it with what you have in Clark's car?"

"I think so. I tried to bring everything with us. It's all in the trunk. I'll have to be really close, though."

"How long to get ready?" Clark asked.

"I don't know. An hour or maybe two if it all comes together right."

"Take Miranda and go out to the car. Get it ready to go," Clark said. He turned to Quinn. "You sure about this? We could try to break through."

"No, they'd see us coming and do something to Filippa and Carina. We have to surprise them or it won't work. I've got this."

"Okay, get yourself ready. I'll go see if the two ladies need help."

Quinn nodded and started scanning the dirt as she walked around, looking for her missing knife. She was pretty sure she was going to need it before the night was through.

CHAPTER TWENTY-FOUR

Quinn shifted in her seat as Clark turned the corner. They'd passed that donut shop at least twenty times now. She glanced over her shoulder.

Taylor sat in the back seat, alternating between fitful bouts of typing on her laptop and pulling wires out of and plugging others into a gray metal case on the seat beside her. The stress creased new lines in her forehead. She'd been working for almost three hours now.

"Taylor," Clark barked. "How's it coming? People's lives are at stake here."

"Clark, if you ask me that one more time, I'm going to jam this laptop so far up your—"

"Hey, you two," Miranda soothed. "Nobody gets saved if we can't get the job done because we're bickering between ourselves. Taylor is well aware of the situation, Clark. Remember, she's been in there, and by herself."

Quinn nodded but kept her mouth shut. Her own anxiety was more likely to make her say something inappropriate, just like Clark did. Miranda had done a decent job of defusing things so far, but even she seemed to be running out of patience.

The plan had the four of them circling the building from two blocks away to ensure they weren't seen by any of the guards or cameras since it wouldn't do to alert their enemies to how close they were. The circuit took at least five minutes to complete. After the tenth trip around, impatience had set in.

Quinn caught herself tapping a beat with her fingers on the dashboard, and she pulled her hand back to her lap. Taylor had snarled at her once already for that particular distraction.

Taylor snapped her fingers, saying, "I think…"

Quinn turned to see what her friend had done. "What?"

"Huh?" Taylor looked up, puzzled.

"What do you think?"

"Oh, yeah. I'm running a test. I think I managed to bypass the key parts of the system tied to the larger version of this gear back at home. If this works, we're ready to go."

That perked up everyone. Miranda flexed her fingers and sat up straighter in her seat. Clark checked the rearview mirror as he drove, looking at Taylor behind him.

The tech witch fist-pumped and looked at Quinn. "Got it. Get yourself set up. We're ready to go."

"No issues?" Miranda asked.

"Nope. The transition is going to be rockier than usual, but other than that, I'm sure we can get you into the building. It helps that I've been there. From this close, I can send you directly where we need to, so we bypass all the security downstairs."

Clark shook his head. "We need her to be where she can shut down the security camera systems."

"I can talk her through that from out here. She should be able to do it from any of the connected terminals used by the stock traders."

Quinn gave a half-smile. She wasn't comfortable with anything beyond the basics of computers. If she hadn't had a friend like Taylor, she'd have been useless with them. Taylor's patient sessions with her had made her better, but only a little. Hacking anything that didn't require a blade of some kind was not going to happen.

Taylor must have seen Quinn's reaction and smiled. "You don't have anything to worry about. You'll have your earpiece, and I'm sending you with this." She produced a small thumb drive from her pocket. "It'll help with the process and do most of the work for you."

"If you say so." Quinn took the silver flash drive and slid it into her back pocket. "Should I get the VR gear on?"

"Yeah, I'm ready to go." Taylor smiled. "Clark, I need you to pull over. I have to be stationary for a few minutes until she's fully transitioned into the system."

The hunter nodded and pulled over to the curb. He slid the gear lever into Park and twisted in his seat, watching the other three as they prepped to send Quinn in. He tapped Quinn's shoulder and said, "Take the security system down, then meet us downstairs as we come in. Don't try to find the princesses on your own. You're in no way ready to take on a mature vampire yet."

"I'll be careful."

"Good."

Taylor raised a hand. "I'm ready to count her in. Miranda, how about you?"

"The spell is the same from my end, right?"

Taylor nodded.

"Then I'm all set."

Quinn settled back in her seat and pulled the VR visor down over her eyes. Her earpiece was already in place, and she reached over to check on her weapon. The Bowie was beneath her right arm. All she could do now was wait.

"Counting down now," Taylor said.

Miranda started a low chant, no louder to Quinn than a distant murmur.

Taylor's voice came through loud and clear. "Ten, nine, eight, seven..."

A searing pain blasted through Quinn's brain so intense she almost called out for them to stop. Taylor said this transition would be rougher, but this...

"Four, three, two, one."

The familiar falling sensation hit Quinn like a sledge-hammer, and darkness closed around her. She welcomed it. At least the massive headache would end soon.

Quinn heard someone laughing, sounding almost maniacal to her ears, then she realized it was her. Before she could stop, she fell into unconsciousness.

CHAPTER TWENTY-FIVE

Quinn woke up with a jolt. This time, she didn't have time to look for a convenient spot to throw up. She didn't even crouch. She woke up vomiting and bent over immediately as she started coughing and choking.

The nausea passed and Quinn spat on the linoleum floor, trying to clear her mouth. Luckily for her, there was no one else in the room in which she found herself. She wished she had a water bottle to rinse her mouth.

Quinn looked around, taking in the room in which she'd landed. Tall filing cabinets lined the walls. A large copy machine or something like it stood in the corner by the closed door. There was a water cooler beside the hulking device.

She went to it, pulled one of the paper cups from the dispenser, and filled it. She swirled the water around her mouth and spat in the nearby trash can, following it with the crumpled paper cup.

Time to get to work.

Taylor had described this place from her earlier foray here, and Quinn realized she'd landed precisely where she was supposed to.

She tapped her earpiece with a finger. "Taylor, I'm here. I'm in the filing room."

"Good. When I didn't hear from you right away, I was worried."

"You warned me it was going to be rough, but I'm okay now." Quinn reached into her pocket and pulled out the thumb drive. "I've got the drive, and I'm ready to go. What's next?"

"Go out the door. There's a long hall. I don't think there'll be anyone around at this time of night, but there could be, so be careful."

Clark's voice came over the earpiece. Taylor must have it on speaker in the car. "It's the lair of a master vampire. There's someone up right now for sure. Be careful."

"Should I try to find a piece of wood and make a stake or something?"

"Your Bowie will do the trick. A thrust to the heart or brain with silver will disable him for at least a few hours. If we need to, we can stake him later. Try to avoid that Handon guy if possible. Vamps have powers of their own, and they're even stronger than the demon-kinder."

"Good to know, thanks. Taylor, after the hall, where do I go?"

"There's a room full of cubicles with computer terminals. Pick one of the terminals and plug the drive in, then call me back."

Quinn tapped her earpiece to clear the connection and crossed the room to the door. Drawing the shadows around her, Quinn whispered, "Mist." The fuzzy haze around her vision came into view, and she pulled the door open. She'd be nearly invisible in case anyone was up and about.

The sound of several voices met her from down the hallway. She couldn't make out any words, but there were two or three people in the cubicles in the room at the end of the corridor.

Opening her mic, Quinn said, "Taylor. There are people here. The overhead lights are out, but it looks like some of the cubicles are lit up and occupied." She moved forward a bit farther to look around, then backed up before speaking. "Looks like three have desk lamps on with people at work."

Miranda said. "Taylor, it's a stock-trading firm. The international markets in places like China and Japan are open right now. They might be ordinary folks working."

Taylor said, "I agree with Miranda. Also, those folks were under a spell or trance or something when I was there. They paid no attention to me. I think the vamp upstairs did something to them. Just try to find a cubicle far away from them in the corner, then be quiet and I'll get you into the system."

"I hope you're right about this, Taylor."

Quinn cut the mic and started back to the trading room. She was confident they couldn't see her, but it nonetheless made her nervous.

The people working were clustered together in the center of the room. She slipped into the corner cubicle next to the corridor. She'd still be several rows away the rest. If she whispered, they wouldn't hear her over their own conversations.

Once she had seated herself in the swivel chair behind the desk, Quinn bent down and looked for a computer hub or tower into which she could insert the drive.

"Taylor. There's no computer here. Just a monitor, a keyboard, and the flat finger-thingie you use to move around the screen."

"That's a trackpad, Quinn." Taylor corrected.

"Whatever. I looked under the desk. There's nothing that looks big enough to be a computer system."

"That's all right. They're all networked together to make one big computer. Look under the desk again and see if you see a network hub with an ethernet plug in both ends."

"A what?"

"Oh, my God, Quinn. How can you be a digital native and not know this stuff? It looks like a phone jack for an old landline, sort of."

"Oh, that thing. Why didn't you say so?" Quinn smiled at the exasperated sigh she got in reply.

She examined the small box under the desk with the networking cables coming into it. The computer ports for the drive Taylor had given her were there. "I see a plug that'll fit. Plug it in there?"

"Yes. Then sit up and power on the monitor. It should just take tapping a key or two or moving your finger on the trackpad."

Quinn plugged the thumb drive into the slot and slid her forefinger across the smooth metal of the trackpad. The blue-white light of the screen glowed. She glanced over her shoulder to see if anyone had seen the glow now coming from her cubicle. No one appeared to have noticed.

Turning back, she whispered, "Now what? The drive is in and the screen is lit. There's a box on the screen with my name on it."

Taylor chuckled. "I tried to keep it simple for you. Just move the cursor over the button that says, 'Quinn Click Here' and click on it. Then sit back and wait while I do my mojo from here."

Quinn did as she was told, then asked, "Can I power down the monitor while I wait?"

"No. That might cut off my access. Don't worry, it won't take long."

Taylor started humming over the open connection. She always did that while she worked. It wouldn't be that bad, but the poor girl was pretty near tone-deaf. Quinn leaned back in her seat, tried to ignore the atonal drone in her ear, and waited for Taylor to do whatever it was she needed to do.

After a minute or so, Quinn cut the connection. She couldn't take it anymore. Taylor could just call her back. Craning her neck over the top of the cubicle, Quinn looked around and saw that the three traders were still at work.

A chime across the room sounded . It was distant, and she probably wouldn't have heard it if she hadn't been directing her huntress senses to listen in to the traders nearby.

Quinn tried to localize it and realized it came from outside the trading room's main entrance. Taylor had said there was a lobby with a bank of elevators outside.

More voices drifted her way, then the lobby doors opened.

Quinn ducked and tapped her earpiece, whispering, "Someone's coming, Taylor. How much longer?"

"Don't let them see the screen. Whoever it is will know what you're doing right away and warn someone."

Quinn cringed. She was afraid of that. Then she got a whiff of stale, wet dog. At least one of the newcomers was a werewolf.

She drew her Bowie, crouching and weaving through the cubicles toward the long corridor. As she made her way across the room, Quinn listened and tried to filter out the stock traders' voices so she could hear the ones who'd just arrived.

"...I don't see why? It's just busywork."

"You wanna go argue with the boss, Barry?"

"No, but it's a waste to search every floor every hour just to keep the boss's friend happy. We can secure this place just fine from the entrances down on the ground floor."

"Just do your job. Walk through and check out this end while I go check the rest of the floor. I'll meet you back upstairs."

The lobby door clicked shut as the other one left Barry in here alone. Quinn heard him grumbling as he started down the row of cubicles. She wanted him to be as far from the lobby door as possible before she attacked. She ducked into a cubicle in the row right next to the hallway leading back to the file room and waited under the desk.

A shadow passed, accompanied by idle whistling.

Peeking around the cubicle wall, Quinn watched as a

large man walked down the hall to the file room. He was going to wonder who'd puked back there.

Crouching, Quinn darted out and padded down the hall, following the guard.

He entered the room and flipped on the lights. "Gah, it smells awful in here. Aw, jeez, seriously? Who makes a mess like this and doesn't clean it up?"

Quinn raced up behind the guard before he could turn around. Just before she hit him, she said, "Me."

She realized it was foolish to announce her presence like that, but she hadn't counted on his reaction speed being as good as it was. Because she wasn't enhancing her strength or speed at the moment, the guard twisted out of the way and dodged her knife thrust.

He snarled in pain as the tip of the Bowie scored a shallow slash across his side. He returned the attack with a strike of his own, his fingers sprouting claws.

Quinn brought her arm up to block the incoming blow. Luckily, her leather jacket caught the worst of the sharp claws extending from Barry's hand, but the attack still sent her reeling across the room to slam into the filing cabinets.

Quinn rolled to the side and jumped back to her feet, expecting a followup attack at any instant. Instead, she watched in horror as Barry completed the transformation from human to full bipedal werewolf form. She'd never seen the change before in bright light like this.

He snarled something that might have been words, but she couldn't understand them.

"Come over here. Let's see if you're any better than the friends of yours I killed the other night downstairs."

The creature's eyes widened, then he charged, clawed hands raised, his snarling jaws open to snap at her.

Quinn didn't make the same mistake she'd made the last time. Dialing up her strength and reaction speed from her stamina, she ducked under the swinging arms.

Her Bowie was out of position for a return strike, but she did punch forward with her other hand. It landed with enough force to knock the wolfman back before he could bite her. Clark had said she was immune to becoming a shifter. That didn't mean she wasn't worried that once those jaws closed on her, she'd have trouble getting away.

This guy was way bigger than the other werewolves she fought downstairs. Quinn wondered if the others were younger or juniors.

Now wasn't the time to try to ask, though. The wolf bounded at her again. This time, a slashing blow caught her right arm, ripping through her jacket and scoring deep, bloody, claw marks from her shoulder to her elbow.

Trying to ignore the fiery pain from the hit, Quinn slashed out with her knife and got in a shot of her own, cutting open a gash in his thigh with the silver-infused knife.

He howled and tried to close the wound and staunch the bleeding with one hairy hand while swinging at Quinn with the other.

With both of them wounded, she figured it wouldn't be long before one of them was down for the count. The next solid hit would probably decide things.

Knowing this, Quinn took a chance. She feinted an attack to her right, drawing the werewolf to step in that direction. Then, she ran left, leaping up sideways and running up along the face of the filing cabinets for a few steps.

This move allowed her to push off and land behind her adversary with her blade extended. Crouching then lunging forward, she pushed the Bowie forward into the hairy thing's back. The knife's tip grated up across its ribs, before slipping between two of them. It plunged home into one of the werewolf's lungs from behind.

The painful howl turned into a gurgling sound as frothy pink bubbles came from the werewolf's mouth. He turned and tried to take a half-strength swipe at her.

She dodged backward with ease and watched him fall over to the floor. He tried to rise once and then was still.

Quinn twisted her head as she tried to see how bad her shoulder was. It hurt a lot, especially when she moved. She flexed her fingers a few times to see if she could still use them. There didn't appear to be any permanent damage, but she wasn't at a hundred percent. She left the lights on in the filing room but shut the door. The glow showed under the door. Hopefully, if Barry's partner decided to come looking for him, it would serve to draw the other werewolf down that way where she could get behind him from out in the trading area.

She moved back out to the cubicles. The three guys hard at work in the middle of the room showed no signs of having heard the howling and fighting just down the hall from them.

Taylor was right. The vampire had them under some sort of mind control. Their focus never seemed to waver from their screens or their phone calls. Quinn moved back to the corner cubicle and tapped her earpiece. "Taylor, you done yet?"

"I just finished. Where'd you go?"

"Two guards came down to check the area. One of them went back this way."

Taylor asked, "Did you get him?"

"One of them. The other one is checking the rest of this floor. I don't know how much time I have until he comes back."

"This won't take long. I've already selected the cameras I want you to freeze. All you have to do is click on the ones I've highlighted for you in the system. It won't let me do it remotely. Make sure nothing is in the image when you freeze it. Freeze all five of the selected cameras on your end, and then you can shut off the monitor."

Quinn did as she was told until all the selected cameras were frozen.

"I'm finished."

Clark's voice answered. "Okay, hide on that floor, and we'll come to you. Then we can all go search for Filippa and Carina."

"Got it," Quinn replied, switching off the monitor and moving back to the end of the cubicle row. She needed to be ready to take care of Barry's partner if he came back. Hopefully, her friends wouldn't take too long. She wasn't feeling very patient right now.

CHAPTER TWENTY-SIX

Clark checked his watch as he drove around their circuit for what felt like the hundredth time. The sun would be up in a few hours. They needed to hurry up and get this done.

He listened as Taylor gave Quinn the final instructions to shut down the cameras. He added, "Okay, hide on that floor, and we'll come to you. Then we can all go search for Filippa and Carina."

"Got it," Quinn replied.

He hoped she listened to instructions for once. She wasn't prepared to take on a vampire with the kind of power this one probably had. Add in the demon-kinder and a rogue pack of werewolves, and she'd be in way over her head.

He pulled the car into a parking space along the curb. They'd be gone before the seven AM limitation on the No Parking sign.

"Miranda, you come with me. Taylor, stay here and take care of getting Quinn out of there if you have to.

The tech witch held up her phone. "I've tapped the whole system into a custom app I built here. I can control the whole thing from any mobile device loaded with the app."

"No," Clark said.

"What do you mean, 'no?'"

"Just what I said. You'll only get in the way in there. I can't be watching out for you while I'm trying to get the job done with Quinn."

"I'm not staying in the car, Clark. My best friend is in there alone. If you leave without me, I'll just follow you. There's going to be more tech in there that you'll need me to deal with, so don't count me out."

Clark grumbled, mostly to himself, "I don't have time for this."

Taylor laid her laptop on the floor of the car with the other gear and covered it with an old blanket. She climbed out of the car and smiled at him as he got out and stood next to her.

Miranda came around from her side and joined them on the sidewalk. "How do we approach this, Clark? Do we just walk up and break in?"

"I'll lead the way. You wait here for now so I can sneak up on any guards still out and about. I'm not sure how many there will be. I'll call you when it's time to enter and go upstairs."

"As long as you remember to call for help if you need it," Miranda said. When Clark opened his mouth to argue, she held up her hand and said, "Our goal is to get all of us inside and upstairs to rescue the princesses. We can't leave Quinn to do it by herself."

Clark thought about explaining how dangerous this was likely to be but decided against it. These two had seen enough by now to know what they were getting into. He hoped that meant they knew this was going to be rough, and they might not all survive. He gave a final nod and turned to head across the street, setting a fast pace.

As he walked, Clark drifted into the shadows, drawing them around himself like a protective cloak. The soft gasp he heard from Taylor behind him brought a smile to his face. She'd never seen him or Quinn use that ability before. It was impressive when you saw it for the first time.

He remembered the first time he'd seen one of his companions shift themselves into the shadows. The memory turned to one of sadness. That friend from his youth was long dead, betrayed by someone he'd trusted, along with all the others in the clan.

Pulling himself back to the job at hand, Clark extended his senses outward, taking in all of his surroundings in the way only a hunter could. His hearing, vision, sense of smell, and even his taste buds were all amped up to a new level of sensitivity. Now, he could detect his enemies before they discovered him. It allowed him to home in on those he tracked.

This time, it allowed him to detect the two shifters sitting on a bench near the front of the building that was their target. He thought they were alone, but he wasn't a hundred percent sure.

He had to be sure these two shifters were the only guards out here. He could take them himself, but he didn't want any surprises.

Moving in silence, he crossed the street to circle around

the two guards. Once he passed by their location, Clark crossed back to the other side, searching for any other guards.

There were none.

Now to take out these two shifters.

Clark took out his phone and texted Miranda and Taylor.

Come on in. Make a little noise to distract the guards out front on your way.

He slid the phone into his pocket and waited. It didn't take long. He heard their voices over the persistent background hum of the city.

The two werewolves, still in human form, heard the two women approaching, too. They stood and moved to the sidewalk so they could see the source of the voices up the street.

Clark smiled as both guards relaxed at the sight of two women walking together toward them. That was all he needed.

Moving in like a lightning strike, he took down the first werewolf from behind before they even knew he was there.

The other shifter was fast, too. He ducked under Clark's return sword stroke and snarled as he punched at the hunter with a fist already shifting form to grow claws.

Clark rolled with the punch, diffusing most but not all of the attack. It hurt, but he'd had worse. Pulling in the follow-through from his sword's swing, he stepped back to strike again before the full transition to wolfman happened.

The shifter had other plans. He turned from Clark and

darted at the two women standing and watching nearby. The shifter had realized they were part of the attack.

"Damn. Watch out!" Clark called to the others. He raced to catch up but knew he'd not get there in time.

He didn't need to.

Miranda and Taylor saw the enraged creature charging at them. The younger of the two drew two silver knives and held them in front of her. At the same time, the witch's hands moved in the air as she wove a spell of some sort.

The shifter almost reached the pair when he yelped, pulled up short as thick vines grew up from cracks in the sidewalk and wrapped around his legs. They continued up to confine his arms, too.

Taylor charged in and stabbed with both hands in a sort of double lunge that struck the creature in the chest. She drew back and moved to thrust again.

Clark's sword struck from behind at the same instant Taylor's blades plunged in for the second time.

The shifter sagged against the vines, wrapped so tightly they held his now-lifeless body up so he couldn't fall.

"Good work, both of you," Clark said. "Come on. Let's get inside."

Taylor wiped her blades on the shredded rags that had been the shifter's t-shirt. She slid her tiny knives back into their sheaths and beamed at him as she walked by, probably because of his compliment.

Clark bit back an additional qualifying comment. That was what he got for being nice.

Miranda slid into step beside him and said, "You should remember both she and Quinn need encouragement from time to time. It doesn't hurt anything when you compliment them."

"You reading my mind now?" Clark replied.

"Didn't have to. It was all over your expression when Taylor went by."

"This is deadly serious work. If we fail, there's no one else around to pick up the slack. There's no room for coddling anyone."

"All the more reason to make sure we keep this team together," Miranda said. "As strange as it is having all of us, with our various backgrounds, together in one team, it seems to work. We all complement the skills of the others in a way that almost seems preordained."

Clark shook his head. "If this is all part of some grand plan, it would've made a lot more sense to have saved the hunter clans twenty years ago. We are way too little, too late."

Taylor had reached the front doors ahead of them and pulled one of them open for them.

Clark nodded a thank you and stepped inside.

Miranda followed, then her hand snapped out to grab his shoulder. "Stop, there are wards in here. I didn't pick up on them from outside. Don't move."

"What kind of wards?" Clark asked. He shifted his eyes into the limited amount of the magical spectrum he could see as he scanned the room. "I can't see anything."

"Neither can I, not with my eyes, but some sort of magic is in play here. It's connected to something or someone on one of the floors above us."

"Can you dispel it or defuse it from doing whatever it's

supposed to do? I don't want to get fried by a rain of fire or something like that."

Miranda paused for a few seconds before she answered. "If I dispel it, whoever is connected will surely know and wonder who shut it down. I can try to create a sort of bubble around us that keeps it from activating, at least in theory. I've never done anything like that before."

Taylor leaned in from behind them, still holding the door partially open. "Maybe we should just dash across to the elevators and hope for the best. It might just be a warning spell or something, in which case whoever cast it already knows we're here."

"Let's hope not, kid," Clark said. "Otherwise, we're going to be facing a lot more than a few werewolves up there. I'd like to get in, locate the Fae princesses, and get out without any more fighting."

Based on the way her shoulders sagged a little, Taylor had anticipated more action. She didn't understand how bad this could get.

"Cast the bubble thing," Clark said. "Let's get going."

Miranda's lips moved as she spoke the spell while weaving her hands and fingers in an intricate circular pattern in the air just inside the doorway.

After about ten seconds, she held her hands up in front of her at shoulder height, palm out. She glanced at Clark and nodded.

Taking a deep breath as if he were about to plunge underwater, Clark strode into the lobby. He didn't feel or sense anything to indicate they'd tripped an alarm.

He gestured to Miranda, who was right behind him,

and to Taylor, who was behind her. "Stay close together and keep your eyes open."

The trio crossed the spacious lobby to the stairwell by the elevators. A hint of optimism Clark hadn't felt for a long time crept into the back of his mind. The unlikely team he and the others had formed since he'd discovered Quinn reminded him of times, years before when he hadn't been so alone in the world.

Clark allowed himself to relax just a little, relying on Miranda's spell to both protect them and provide a hint of warning.

Unfortunately, the spell was able to do neither, at least not in time.

The three of them passed by the security desk. Clark had started reaching for the stairwell door when all four elevators behind them opened simultaneously.

Taylor shouted, "Watch out."

Clark turned, reaching for the short sword at his waist. He never got the chance to draw it. Four enormous were-wolves piled on top of him, driving him to his knees and then forward onto the floor.

He managed to roll to one side and get one arm up to block the incoming blows from the clawed hands reaching in at him. He heard Taylor scream twice. Then she fell silent. He didn't know about Miranda, but she was surely down as well.

Preparing himself to fight to the last breath, Clark punched outward while he tried to dislodge the weight of the creatures atop him. Their claws and fangs had penetrated his meager defenses, and he started to weaken.

His balled fist met the jaw of one of the creatures, the

one that had bent in to try to get to his throat. His last ounce of enhanced hunter strength went into the final desperate attack. The werewolf's head snapped back from the strike, and his eyes lost focus as he was knocked out.

"Stop!" There was no mistaking the command in the strange, amplified voice coming through the speakers in the ceiling. "Take them alive and bring them to me. I want to meet the ones who've done so much to thwart my plans."

The clawed hands stopped trying to rip him apart, instead grabbing his arms and pinning them to his sides as the shifters lifted him to his feet. Clark struggled to kick those holding him, then something struck his head from behind twice in rapid succession. Clark's part of this fight ended in unconsciousness.

CHAPTER TWENTY-SEVEN

Quinn crouched beneath the desk in the corner cubicle. She didn't know how long she'd been waiting, but it shouldn't have taken this long to come up here and find her. Taylor knew her way around, after all.

She reached up and tapped the earpiece, waited a few seconds, and pressed it again.

Nothing.

Taking the apparatus off, Quinn checked to make sure it still had power.

The tiny green light on the inside surface of the device indicated it was still on and had enough battery life left to be working. Beyond that, she didn't know what to do. Quinn's experience with technology was limited to turning things on and off when they stopped working.

She did that now, cycling the tiny device's battery pack off and back on.

The second time she did, the light blinked twice, and

she picked up a faint chirp. She quickly slipped the earpiece into place again.

"Taylor, where are you guys?"

"Alas, I'm sorry to say they will not be joining you at this time."

Whoever that was, it wasn't Taylor. The man's voice, even over the electronic connection, carried weight and authority.

"Who are you?"

"I guess you could say I'm your host, Quinn. That's your name, is it not? Right now, I'd like to extend an invitation to come up to the twelfth floor and join me. Your friends are all here. I'm sure they'd like to see you. We can discuss the inconvenience you've caused me when you get here."

"How do I know you won't kill me or that my friends aren't dead?"

"You don't, my dear. For now, though, all I want to do is talk. I've heard some things about you, and I'd like to chat. I promise you'll not be harmed until we've finished our conversation."

"And if I don't come up and join you?"

"Then I'll kill your friends one at a time until you do. Please don't keep me waiting. I'm not a patient man."

The line went dead with a single click.

Damn, now what?

She wasn't at a hundred percent right now. The werewolf earlier had injured her arm and shoulder. She could move it, but the wound was bad enough that she wasn't sure she'd survive another fight. That would be doubly true in a battle where she took on an ancient vampire, in addition to his werewolf minions. Plus, Myles, Cindy, and the rest of the VirSync cult had to be around here somewhere, too. That was a lot to face down on her own.

But there was no way she'd leave her friends up there to die. She had to try to free them. Steeling herself, Quinn got up and walked back to the entrance to the trading offices. Soon she stood by the elevator and pressed the up button.

The doors opened right away to reveal two giant werewolves, one in each of the back corners of the elevator. The one on the left gestured to the floor in the center of the car.

Quinn nodded. If they'd wanted to kill her, they could've attacked her as soon as the doors opened.

"Hi, guys. I guess you're my escorts." Quinn forced a smile and stepped in. "I don't suppose you'd like to tell me what to expect upstairs?"

A deep, growling chuckle was her only answer.

"Oh, well, then, let's just get this over with." She reached over and punched the button for the twelfth floor and turned away from the werewolves, despite the hair standing up on the back of her neck. She had to give them the idea she knew something they didn't. Putting on an amused smile, Quinn hummed a bit of one of her favorite songs while she waited for the doors to open again. Her only defense at this point was bravado.

It wasn't a long trip up to the next floor. The doors slid back to reveal Cindy, Myles Hickman, and several hulking men. Judging by the smell, they were werewolf pack members. The largest of them might even be the leader of the rogue pack. She wasn't really sure how such things worked. She'd have to remember to ask Clark about it later.

If there was a later.

"Good morning, Quinn," Myles said. "I'm so glad you saved us the trouble of coming down to bring you in."

"I didn't really have a choice, did I?"

"No, I guess you didn't." Myles pointed at her leg. "Cindy said your leg was quite seriously injured during your last encounter. It seems that was not the case."

Quinn shrugged. "I don't know what to tell you. Maybe your pet demon girl isn't trustworthy. As you can see, my leg is just fine."

"Your arm is not, however," Cindy snarled. "I'm glad to see that idiot Barry managed to hurt you before you killed him, at least. I assume you're the reason he didn't return from his patrol?"

Quinn nodded. "He got in the way. I did to him what I do to all those who get in my way. You both should remember that."

Myles laughed and said. "I think you have used up whatever luck you might have had tonight, girl. I wanted to go down there and kill you myself, but John has other plans. He wanted to meet this huntress he's been hearing so much about."

"Well, let's not keep him waiting. I have things to do."

"What might that be?" Myles asked. "Surely you don't think you're leaving this place alive, do you?"

"People have tried killing me before. It hasn't stuck yet."

Myles didn't reply. Instead, he gave her a toothy grin as he gestured for her to walk beside him. Quinn fell into place, with Cindy and the four werewolves following her and Myles.

She resisted the urge to try to reach back to scratch the

persistent itch between her shoulder blades that came from having so many enemies at her back.

Myles led her to a dark-paneled room with a long wooden conference table. At the far end sat a tall, thin man who had to be the vampire, John Handon. In the first three seats to the vampire's left sat Clark, Miranda, and Taylor. Their arms were bound to the arms of the wooden chairs in which they sat. All three were gagged, as well.

They stared at her as she entered. There was fear in Miranda's and Taylor's faces, and anger flared in Clark's dark eyes.

"Ah, Quinn. So good of you to join us." The vampire pointed at her arm, bloody and hanging at her side. He licked his lips as if tasting the scent of blood in the air with a flick of his tongue. "You didn't tell us you were injured."

"It's a scratch. I'll be good as new before you know it."

The vampire chuckled, although there was no light or mirth in his eyes. "My dear, I'd heard somehow the hunter clans were trying to re-establish themselves, despite being nearly wiped out decades ago. Clearly, the report I received about the demise of the clans was incomplete. Unless you're not who you seem to be?"

"The hunter clans are dead and gone, Handon. I'm the start of something different. I'm a huntress. If you don't let my friends go, I'll be your worst nightmare." Quinn had to keep him talking while she worked to come up with a solution. There had to be a way out of this. She was no quitter.

Handon stroked his chin for a second, then said. "You might not be the real thing, but you have mastered the hubris the hunters and others of that ilk displayed for so long. Too bad your boastful nature is misplaced." He gestured, and two of the werewolves behind Quinn moved up and grabbed her.

Quinn let out an involuntary gasp as the one on her right dug his elongated nails into the open wounds on her arm. Her vision clouded with pain, and she struggled to hold on as things grayed out for a few seconds. She regained control of her wobbly knees and stared back at Handon, matching him glare for glare. She had to remain focused, or she'd never get out of here or rescue her friends. The first task was to keep the vampire talking.

Quinn glanced around the conference room. "What did you do to the two fae princesses? I'm surprised you don't have them trussed up here, too."

Handon laughed, throwing his head back, mouth open. His elongated canines were visible. "My poor, foolish girl, the capture of the fae was a ploy to demonstrate the power I hold in this region. It was done to gain a psychological advantage, nothing more. We reached an accommodation with the others soon after they were taken. I released the two fairies and allowed them to return to their little festival before you arrived."

Quinn's heart sank. They'd gone to all this trouble for nothing. She fumbled in her mind for something to say in response. In the end, all she did was glare at Handon and say, "Well, that's one less thing I have to do after I finish dealing with you."

The vampire glided around the table, shaking his head as he held Quinn's gaze. His hand rode along the tops of the chairs behind her seated friends. "You fail to realize the seriousness of your plight, Quinn. I sense your thoughts. You still think you can fight your way out of here."

He paused, tapping a finger on his chin in thought. "Perhaps you need a lesson to help you understand who is in charge here, Huntress." He managed to turn the title into a sneer. "None of you will be leaving here alive. I have kept you all around this long to find out how you've managed to counter my underlings' plans."

He nodded at Myles and Cindy, who were now standing off to the side near the head of the conference table. Quinn caught the hint of fear in Myles's eyes when Handon referred to him, and a brief moment of satisfaction coursed through her. She let Myles's discomfort fuel the smile on her face, refusing to surrender or admit defeat.

The vampire noticed her response because he turned instead of continuing around the table in her direction. "Yes, I think an object lesson is in order. I believe you should learn first-hand what happens to those who defy me."

He walked back behind Taylor, Miranda, and Clark, this time letting his fingers hover in the air above them, pausing for a moment over each of them. In each case, he reached down and tapped his forefinger on their heads.

Taylor jerked her head to try to avoid his touch. Miranda stared straight ahead and didn't respond. Clark stared upward as the vampire walked behind him as if he were tracking Handon's position, even though he couldn't see him directly.

A desperate idea popped into Quinn's mind. She silently brought up her HUD map of the building and the surrounding block. She was about to zoom in on her location on the map when Handon reversed his direction.

He gave her the same mirthless smile and went to stand behind Miranda.

With speed only a supernatural creature could display, he grabbed Miranda by her hair, bending her head back until she screamed in pain through the gag.

"No…" Quinn began.

Before she could finish her plea, Handon drew his index finger across the witch's throat. His claw-like fingernail, filed to a point, painted a thin line of red as it passed over the witch's skin.

At first, Quinn thought it was just a flesh wound, meant only to scare them.

She was wrong.

The vampire's fingernail must've been razor-sharp. The incision he made across Miranda's throat was thin because it was precise. The rapid flow of blood from the severed jugular vein stained her neck and shoulders with dark red blood as she struggled wide-eyed for a few seconds against the hand holding her head in place.

Quinn used her augmented strength to pull with all her remaining might against the two werewolves holding her. They were ready for her, and the other two shifters came forward to join their packmates in holding her still. Their grips grew tighter as she struggled in place.

Her stamina drained quickly as she kept fighting, trying to do something—anything—to reach her friend and save her. Her struggles soon left her depleted and weakened to the point where she could barely stand. Quinn never took her eyes off Miranda, though. She saw the moment the light dimmed in the witch's eyes as she slipped away, death taking her.

Quinn choked back a sob, saying, "You didn't have to do that."

"Probably not. It was a waste of a good meal, at the very least. I thought you needed proof I was serious. The only thing you control right now is whether I kill you and your friends fast or slowly. It's up to you, and only you."

"What do you want to know?"

"I want you to tell me who sent you. There's no way you infiltrated my operation at VirSync by accident. *Who sent you?* What other plans do they have? Tell me that, and I'll make your deaths as fast as the witch's. Fail, and I'll take each of your friends apart piece by piece while you watch."

He moved behind Taylor, grabbing her by the hair with one hand to hold her still while he tugged her right ear.

Taylor struggled and screamed in anger through her gag.

"Shall we start with this little tidbit first?" He lifted the ear, pulling hard enough to cause Taylor to try to rise in her seat to release the tension.

Quinn's false bravado drained away as despair filled her in a sudden rush. Handon was right. He held all the cards and was playing a game far above everything she and Clark had been trying to do. Now he thought she was part of some sort of conspiracy, and she couldn't prove him wrong. She had no way to satisfy that assumption. There was nothing she could do to stop him from pulling apart her best friend one piece at a time.

She stared forward, her weakened state causing her eyes to lose focus a little so that the HUD map, still up in her mind, and the room in front of her kept switching places as if they were two layers of transparent film.

A faint gold line at the edge of the map twinkled as it moved from foreground to background, the flickering caused by the way her vision swam. It caught her attention as if trying to tell her something.

Then she knew what it meant.

Quinn closed her eyes and drew upon the last of her reserves. She weakened further, sagging against the two pairs of strong hands that held her.

The vampire lord laughed at what he assumed was his victory.

Focusing inward, Quinn concentrated on the place her amulet rested. All the danger and malicious magic around her chilled the silver to an icy lump on her chest.

She ignored that, instead using the magic within it, and within herself, to expand her awareness outward until she reached the edge of the map and the flickering gold line.

This had to work.

It was the only chance any of them had.

CHAPTER TWENTY-EIGHT

Quinn's awareness reached out to the distant ley line. When she'd done this before, it hadn't required so much effort on her part. This time, no matter how hard she tried, the line seemed just out of reach.

Her mind churned through options, trying everything she could think of to grab the energy pulsing past the location twelve stories below.

Below.

Was the difficulty tied to her elevation? When she did this back at the farmhouse, she'd been in the basement, actually underground. If ley lines were tied to the earth and the power within it, then it would make sense that proximity to the ground would have something to do with access to that power.

Outside the internal struggle Quinn waged, Handon's voice reached her consciousness. "I tire of your delays in answering me, Huntress. Perhaps you need a further example to be made of your companions?"

Taylor shrieked, and Quinn's eye's popped open. "No, don't. I can't think straight. I've lost a lot of blood."

The vampire had sliced open the skin in front of Taylor's ear and was pulling on the lobe and stretching the three-inch incision open as blood flowed down her best friend's cheek to her neck.

"Tell me who sent you. Tell me what their plans are, or she'll lose more than her ear."

Quinn stared at Handon's extended finger as he lowered it to rest on Taylor's neck. Anger fueled her, along with fear for her friend's life.

At the base of the building, Quinn's extended awareness pulled the ley line's power, using every last ounce of magical energy stored within her amulet.

The pressure on her chest increased, and the cold became so intense, it seared into her skin. Quinn didn't care. In a sudden, final lunge with her awareness, she managed to peel away a strip of gold energy as she'd done before.

The bar of light bent in her direction on the HUD and surged upward as it found its way to the building's concrete and steel foundation. The metal beams facilitated the transfer of energy up to her the same way it would dissipate a lightning strike from above.

Quinn drank in the power when it reached her at last. She ignored the pain in her tortured muscles as she convulsed from the energy coursing through her.

The injured arm repaired itself, tissue and bone knitting together in an instant. Quinn's last shred of consciousness worked to contain the energy surge within her core, hiding any sign of what she did. She knew how the visible outward glow she'd evidenced back at the farmhouse would give away her rejuvenation.

She pulled in more power, drinking the energy in pulsing bursts as if she were gulping mouthfuls of water from a hose. At last, she could hold no more.

Quinn shifted her gaze from Taylor's bloody neck and ear, raising her eyes to lock her gaze with Handon's.

At first, he met her gaze with a steely fire of his own, trying to force his vampiric glamour on her to control her actions and command answers to his questions. Then the look in his eyes shifted to puzzlement.

"Girl, whatever you're thinking, you have no way out of this. The rest of you will die, no matter what you think you can do. Don't try anything foolish."

The extended clawed finger resting on Taylor's neck twitched as he began to carry out his earlier threat.

Like the snapping rebound of a bungee cord, Quinn released the force within her all at once. She hoped she was right about what she was about to do because she'd only get one chance at this.

Quinn let out the hidden glow within her.

Many things happened at once.

Brilliant blue-white light flared from every bit of her exposed skin, even her eyes.

The vampire let go of Taylor and raised both hands to shield his face as he cried out in pain. Everywhere the light touched him, his skin sizzled and smoked under the onslaught of energy surging from Quinn's body.

At the same moment, she jerked her shoulders and arms inward, pulling at the two werewolves holding her wrists. This time, she pulled free of the shifters' grasp with ease, their claws no longer able to grip her.

Filled with more power than she'd held, Quinn twisted in place. They'd been so sure of themselves, they hadn't bothered searching or disarming her. She yanked her Bowie free of its hidden sheath beneath her jacket.

Continuing the arc of drawing the blade, she slashed the neck of shifter on her left, nearly decapitating him with a single blow. His death throes blocked the other shifter on that side.

The two werewolves on her right slashed her with their clawed hands. Both connected, one on her arm, and the other raking across her ribs.

Quinn ignored the pain of the new injuries, a sort of berserker rage filling her. Spinning, she landed a kick that sent the first werewolf on the right flying back to slam into the wood paneling on the conference room wall.

She landed on her feet, lunging forward and thrusting her blade deep into another shifter's chest.

He clutched the blade as it slid free, trying to staunch the flow of blood. He'd be dead soon enough.

The final shifter backed up and through the open door, his hands up in surrender.

Quinn knelt and snatched a belt knife from one of the creature's fallen companions. In a fluid arc, her arm extended, flinging the blade into his throat.

The shifter collapsed in a twitching heap to the thick blood-red carpet.

Standing, Quinn turned until she faced Cindy and Myles at the head of the conference table.

The cult leader muttered a few words and extended one

hand in her direction. Jets of fire spread from his fingers and flowed directly at Quinn's head.

She ducked under the fire stream, although the heat burned a few stray hairs on the top of her head. Quinn squeezed her eyes closed to shield them against the superheated air accompanying the jet of flame.

When she stood again, weapon ready, she realized the fire had been more of a diversion than an attack. Myles and Cindy had run around the conference table to join John Handon where he stood in the corner by the door. He'd retreated there after the blast of light. The red and black charred patches on his face and arms stood out in stark contrast to his otherwise pale white skin. Myles and Cindy helped steady him, patting out the smoldering spots on his expensive tailored suit.

Quinn only had a few seconds before her opponents regrouped.

She dove across the table, propelling herself with all the boosted strength and speed granted by the energy surge. With speed and a surety she'd never have managed without the magical enhancement, Quinn slashed to the left and right at the bonds securing her two remaining friends to the chairs.

Clark bounded to his feet, sparing a single saddened glance at Miranda's lifeless body slumped in the chair beside him. He pulled the gag from his mouth and pointed to Handon. "You'll pay for her life with your own evil existence, vampire."

Clark didn't have his sword, but he'd pulled out a push dagger hidden in the buckle of his belt, it's silver alloy blade ready for action.

Quinn regained her feet and joined Taylor on either side of the elder hunter. Taylor held out her fists, having lost her silver knives. Quinn held her Bowie ready and waited for Clark's signal to advance.

Handon managed a raspy laugh, though he was obviously severely injured. Quinn's flare of sunlight, or whatever it was, had done more than just superficial burn damage. "hunter, you are out of your league. I've not survived this long without being prepared for even the most remote possibilities. I have plans for all contingencies."

He pulled his charred hand from a pocket within his suit coat and brought something shiny and golden to his mouth. A thin, high, piercing whistle sounded.

When he brought the whistle down, his cracked and burned lips parted in a smile that exposed his elongated canines. "You'll be a little bit too busy, at least for the time being. Perhaps we'll meet again—if you survive, that is."

A chorus of howls echoed from the darkened area outside the conference room.

As Quinn and the others turned to search for the source, a hidden panel opened. Myles and Cindy rushed the injured vampire to the dark opening beyond and disappeared into the passageway, pulling the secret door closed.

There was no time for Quinn, Clark, or Taylor to go after them. Six werewolves bounded into the room, hunched over to run on all-fours.

"Get behind me and watch Taylor," Quinn called. She charged forward, moving faster than even her own eyes could follow.

Behind her, Clark stepped in front of the tech witch,

brandishing his small push dagger.

Quinn fell back on her carefully honed martial arts instincts and the long hours of training Clark had put her through in the last month. The lessons all came back to her. She spun and twisted through her forms, slashing and thrusting. She executed a series of complementary punches and kicks at the charging werewolves, too.

Two of the beasts fell almost immediately, underestimating her speed and strength in the initial rush to get at their prey.

The other four split up and circled the trio, searching for a break in the huntress' berserker fighting style.

As she twisted and leaped from place to place, driving the shifters back from her friends, Quinn paid little attention to her stamina bar. That was a mistake she discovered when she failed to stop one of the charging werewolves before it could reach out and clamp its jaws down on Taylor's arm.

Taylor screamed. The girl pounded her fist on its head, beating it until Clark dispatched it with a single sweep of his silver push knife.

Quinn didn't have time to dwell on her friend's injury. Two shifters remained and her stamina flashed an ominous dark-red color, which showed it was completely drained.

Her knees quivered beneath her, which she hoped the two shifters didn't see.

Quinn pointed to the door of the conference room, working to steady her voice when it quavered as she spoke. "Leave now, and you'll live to warn your pack. Tell them to return to peaceful coexistence with humanity, or I swear

I'll hunt every last one of them down and turn their pelts into rugs for my lair."

The two remaining werewolves glanced at each other, then back at her.

"I'd listen to her," Clark said, stepping up to stand by her side. "She's the huntress of this clan. She'll not give you a second warning."

The creatures didn't wait to see if Clark was right about the second warning. They turned and scampered from the room, fighting each other to get through the door at the same time.

As soon as they were out of sight, Quinn reached up to steady herself on Clark's shoulder.

"You all right?" he asked.

"I will be. I spent a lot of personal energy just now. I'm going to need a little time to recharge." Quinn looked at the corner where Handon and the others had escaped. "What about them?"

"We'll have to let them get away. We're in no condition to go after anyone right now. The vampire almost certainly had a supply of blood nearby. He'll be on his way to healing himself, and we don't want to be here when he is back up to strength."

Clark pointed to her chest. "You're burned."

Quinn glanced down and gasped. Her amulet had burned a hole through her t-shirt, and it had changed, too. Now it was nothing more than a hunk of melted slag on a chain. It no longer resembled the shiny, engraved oval she'd had since she was left by her parents so long ago.

She lifted it in her fingers, running her thumb over the dull, rounded surface. Her chest wasn't burned beneath it despite what it had done to the shirt's fabric. The power from the ley line had kept her safe from that while it had coursed through her.

Taylor's pained voice broke through Quinn's thoughts. "A little help here. I can't stop the bleeding."

Quinn turned to Taylor, now seated on the floor cradling her injured forearm and trying to press on the savaged skin there to stop the flow of blood from the bite wound.

Quinn tore a strip off the bottom of her t-shirt. She didn't have time to worry about how dirty it might be. She wrapped it around Taylor's arm and pulled it tight, twisting the knot so that the fabric clamped down on the vessels beneath and staunched the flow of blood.

"Clark, you need to get her to a hospital. This needs more attention than you or I can give it."

"What about you?" the hunter asked. He had been untying Miranda's limp body from the chair. He carried her over and laid her down where Taylor sat.

"I'm still in the VR."

Taylor smiled. "That's easy. Clark can just click on the exit sequence button in the app on my phone. You'll pop back into the car right where you left."

"Where are you going to be?" Quinn asked.

"I think I'm going to be unconscious if that's okay." She punctuated the statement by slumping over to lay atop Miranda's body.

"Clark, get her downstairs. I'll get Miranda's body out of here and hidden down by the alley and the loading dock."

"You can barely stand, Quinn. How do you expect to

carry her?"

Quinn smiled. "I'll figure out something. Wait until I send you the recall signal before you summon me back, then I can tell you where Miranda's body is. We can come back for her after we drop Taylor off at the Mercy Hospital ER. It's not too far from here."

Clark nodded and picked up Taylor from the floor. He gave one last look around and then walked from the room back to the elevators.

Quinn waited until he left before she finally let the tears flow. They dripped down her cheeks to fall on the floor as she struggled to drag Miranda's body in the same direction. She wouldn't leave the witch's body here alone. She could at least get the body outside the building. Even if she and Clark couldn't come back, the authorities would eventually find her and give her a burial of some sort.

It took some work, plus the lucky discovery of a mail cart near the elevators, but Quinn got Miranda down to the alley and stashed behind a dumpster. There was no sign of the werewolf pack though she could smell traces of them, especially down by the loading dock.

Quinn stared up and down the alley to mark the position in her mind. She hated to leave Miranda alone there, but she had to get back from the VR system before Taylor's laptop ran out of power. There was no telling what would happen to her if she stayed in here too long.

Quinn pushed the earpiece into place and pressed the button twice in rapid succession. A few seconds later, the familiar swirling blackness and nausea caught her. She fell backward into it, leaving the VR system and its magic behind.

CHAPTER TWENTY-NINE

Quinn dumped a last shovelful of earth over the grave and patted it down with the flat back of the shovel. Clark stood nearby, placing the carved wooden plank at the head end of the mounded earth. He'd worked on it all night and Quinn admired the handiwork he'd displayed. The stylized image represented a tree and leaf motif representing nature and balance.

"I think she'd like it," Quinn said.

"I know she would," Taylor agreed from beside her. She pulled at the sling that held her injured arm and then bent down to lay a small bouquet of wildflowers atop the mound of dirt.

Clark came to stand beside the others and stared down at their handiwork. "We need to get going."

Quinn nodded. "I wish we could stay. It was starting to feel like home, here."

"They know where it is, Quinn," Clark said. "It will only be a matter of time before they come back and look for us."

"I know. It's not like I ever really had a home anyway."

Taylor came over and rested her hand on Quinn's shoulder. "We're a clan, Quinn. Home is wherever we find ourselves."

"Someday, Taylor, I swear we'll have a real place to call home, for us and for the clan."

Clark picked up the shovel and the mallet he'd been using to drive the plank into the dirt. "Until then, let's load up and get out of here."

"Where to?" Taylor asked Clark.

"I have a few places I've set up over the years to hide. The closest one isn't too far from here. Then we can see about finding out what Handon and the others are up to next."

Quinn touched the lump of melted metal that had been her magical amulet. It still hung around her neck on its silver chain, but it wasn't anything but an inert hunk of slag now. There only remained a mirror image of the amulet branded into the center of her chest.

She shook her head. They had all sacrificed so much in the final fight. They'd lost Miranda, and that stung more than what had happened to her amulet. Without the witch's help, Quinn wasn't sure how they were going to be able to fight back when the next time rolled around.

Her fingers closed around the remains of the amulet and squeezed until it hurt. If only she could go back and do something different, find some other way to win that could've saved her friend.

She followed Taylor and Clark back to the car, despair from all her failures in the past week washing over her. She hadn't told Clark the amulet wasn't the only thing she'd lost. Her newfound huntress powers and abilities gained in the past few months had all vanished when she burned out in the fight downtown.

Quinn had prayed as she refilled the grave earlier, seeking guidance from any higher being who would listen. She begged for an answer to what had happened. She hoped for some explanation that would tell her why they had to lose so much.

That was when she'd heard the distant voice calling to her. She told no one about it. The voice was her only hope for redemption, and she'd share it with no one.

Not yet, anyway.

"Be strong, my huntress. Your power is only misplaced. Seek your heritage and restore it from the source."

Quinn expected that to be all there was but this time, the voice was followed by a familiar one.

"The goddess is correct, Quinn," Miranda said. *"Seek out your past. Find your mother, for she can restore everything you desire."*

The End

Quinn has to recover her lost magic and avenge lost friends against the biggest boss yet in Huntress Cadet, book 3 in the Huntress Clan Saga. Coming soon to Amazon and Kindle Unlimited.

Vampire Hunts, Lost Power, and Betrayal.

Huntress Quinn Faust and her friends search for a master vampire in hiding. Her new clan deals with the aftermath of their battle with John Handon and his minions. All the while, Quinn fights for control over her abilities following the destruction of her magical amulet.

A thin glimmer of hope leads them on a quest for ancient Hunter knowledge. Even the intrigue of Fae power struggles won't deter Quinn as she seeks to replace what she lost.

Join Quinn and her Huntress clan as they race against time itself to stop a plot to take over Baltimore's supernatural community.

Available now at Amazon and through Kindle Unlimited

Extreme Medical Services: Medical Care On The Fringes Of Humanity

Monsters, Paramedics, and Street Medicine

New paramedic Dean Flynn is fresh out of the academy.

Then he learns his patients aren't your normal 911 callers.

With patients that are vampires, werewolves, fairies and more, will Dean survive his first days on the new job?

Will his patients?

Come along now with Extreme Medical Services, a supernatural medical thrill-ride with the paramedics of Elk City by best-selling author and real-life paramedic Jamie Davis.

Jump on the ambulance with Dean, Brynne and the rest of the team.

Get the first book in this best-selling service for free at Amazon.com.

I wrote Huntress Apprentice leading into the holiday season and I found myself thinking about family a lot as I put together the next story about Quinn Faust. The search for a family, one that will stand by her through thick and thin, is the driving force in Quinn's life. She'd never had one growing up in foster care and she wants it.

I was a whole lot luckier than Quinn growing up, but family is also a driving force in my life. I realized a lot of what that meant to me as I dealt with the death of two family members as 2019 closed and the holidays approached. The first to pass was my step brother, only a few years older than myself. He died suddenly after a freak work accident. We were never particularly close because our parents married when we were both already adults. But, for both sides of the family, it was important we rallied around his wife, daughter, mother, and brother to show our support.

About a month later, my eldest aunt died after fighting a prolonged illness. Though not as much of a shock, once again, family came into play. Everyone stepped forward to show support, bringing food, attending funeral home viewings, and just about anything else we could think of to help out. This is what my family does for each other in tough times.

In light of my family's challenges over the holidays, I reflected on how loss affected Quinn at the end of Huntress Apprentice, losing a member of her newly assembled clan of close friends. This was the family she'd helped to create and already she'd lost someone. I thought about how she might face this loss in the uncertain future facing her in book 3. Something tells me it's only going to make her stronger.

It is my hope that each of us finds the family that best supports us. For some it will be the family as defined by blood. For others, like Quinn, it will be a family defined by choices we've made. In either case, having the right family around us helps us all become the best we can be. I urge you to seek out the best family for you, either related by blood or among your circle of friends. You never know when you'll need them.

Until next time, Peace.

ABOUT JAMI DAVIS

Jamie Davis is a nurse, retired paramedic, author, and nationally recognized medical educator who began teaching new emergency responders as a training officer for his local EMS program. He loves everything fantasy and sci-fi and especially the places where stories intersect with his love of medicine or gaming.

Jamie lives in a home in the woods in Maryland with his wife, three children, and dog. He is an avid gamer, preferring historical and fantasy miniature gaming, as well as tabletop games. He writes urban and contemporary paranormal fantasy stories, and LitRPG/GameLit, among other things.

He loves hearing from readers and going to cons and events where he meets up with fans. Reach out and say "hi." Visit JamieDavisBooks.com for more books, free offers and more!

My author site is: https://jamiedavisbooks.com

My Facebook group is: https://facebook.com/groups/funfantasyreaders

Twitter — https://twitter.com/podmedic

Instagram — https://instagram.com/podmedic